THE
MARTLEDGE
VARIATIONS

The Martledge Variations

by

Simon Kurt Unsworth

Sunnworth

BLACK SHUCK
SHADOWS

Black Shuck Books
www.BlackShuckBooks.co.uk

First published in the UK by Black Shuck Books, 2018

978-1-913038-12-0

For my Grandma, Hazel, who walked the coffin road in the months before the writing of this collection, and for my Granddad, Barry, who I hope will live forever.

I love you both.

Prologue

Originally, it had been three smaller villages – Upper and Lower Wells, and Martledge – with Upper and Lower Wells being opposite each other on either side of the road and Martledge a mile or so beyond them. The river passed close to Upper Wells' southerly edge before curling away westwards to make its leisurely way through the land on its journey to the sea.

The first official record of the area was in legal documents from the thirteenth century that set out various farm plots and conferred grazing rights and the right to gather wood (with a specific prohibition against using the wood for the purposes of building "structures dedicated to worship or joy"), all granted by the baron of the area to his tenants. A map from the early fourteenth century shows these three farming hamlets, the farms that made them up and the labourers' cottages that surround the farms. Martledge was the largest even then, arranged around a village green on the edge of the wide floodplain that once every few years would disappear under a foot or two of water, but was otherwise good grazing land. Upper Wells was only slightly smaller than Martledge at that point, with Lower Wells straggling behind, mostly inhabited by the poorest of the residents. A single major road, the winding route that crossed the ridge of hills that framed the area and brought trade in and out (and that came later to be named the Baby Way for reasons that were never clear), connected the three places. It dropped from the nearest slope, ran between the Wells and then through to Martledge, before continuing north and running parallel to the river, only shifting direction again two miles beyond when it ran along the edge of the rising land that ended the floodplain and crossed the river by the Failing Bridge. The three hamlets existed together, separate but intertwined, families rarely moving from one to another, but with marriages locking the people to each other in threads like webs. They were farmers and labourers, wives and children. The smithy lived in Upper Wells, the doctor in Martledge. There were midwives in all three hamlets.

People existed. They survived.

Five hundred years after the first mention of them, Martledge had become the most important of the three hamlets. It had a church – St Clements, standing on one side of the village green – that served all three settlements, and whose stained glass windows showed farmhands cowered beneath the gaze of a stern, unforgiving God. Also on the village green were two pubs, the Horse and Jockey and The George, and if worshippers in these two hallowed spaces seemed jollier than those in the church then that was only to be expected. The primary school was on the other side of Martledge, built by the beneficence of the area's major landowner and easily richest resident, Major John Sutton. Most children were schooled little, and were put out to work early.

The Sutton family were successful, not only as landowners taking rents from both residents and working tenants, but also as farmers and investors, and their wealth benefitted the area.

They built more homes to rent to labourers and provided seasonal accommodation, for a price, in wooden sheds that featured flat cots for the men to sleep on but little else in the way of amenities. They set up a series of small subsidiary industries (among them a pottery making bricks and cheap plates, a snuff works creating snuff from imported tobacco and a gunpowder works outside the town) and invested heavily in arms and munitions. In the late nineteenth century they built a second church in Upper Wells, a larger school in Martledge and paid for the development of the first sewers for all three places, draining directly into the river. They were of their time; harsh employers and landlords but fair according to their own codes, no worse than most other rich business families, protecting their own only so far as their own profited them. They were senior investors in a local bank, and lived on the green in a house that had its own orchard, although few fruit were ever produced by its stunted trees.

Over time, the area changed. Martledge spread, row after row of new houses growing back from the green in all directions, turning it first into a village and then, by the late nineteenth century, a town.

The first to go was Lower Wells, which Martledge absorbed just before the Great War. It became little more than a suburb, and although the name Lower Wells remained in use for a few years, by the early thirties it existed only on old maps; Lower Wells was now a part of Martledge.

The second war, and the austerity that followed it, slowed Martledge's growth but in the 60s, as optimism and the economy grew alongside each other, Martledge bloomed again. This time the spread headed north into the farmlands, as well as continuing the inexorable march back towards the hills, swallowing everything as it went. Upper Wells was soon overtaken, becoming first Wells Martledge, then Wells, and finally just another part of Martledge, an area that families moved into where their houses stood on the remnants of farm buildings and fields and the views they offered would have been unrecognisable to the land's previous tenants. By the 1970s, Martledge was a desirable place to live and has remained so ever since; surrounded still by open land yet connected by an improved infrastructure to the nearby cities, it does well for itself. It offers safety, security and enough air to breathe.

So there it is. Martledge, a town now rather than three hamlets. The green remains, the pubs remain, alongside more that have sprouted to fulfil the needs of the greatly increased population. There are more churches, new schools, shops and businesses by the score. The people there are mostly young, starter families, or elderly, some of whom still remember when the crèche over the river was the local Sutton Bank, when Martledge Row (a set of houses just back from the village green) was one wing of the Sutton House, when their parents called part of south Martledge 'Upper Wells'. Martledge has areas of greater wealth (the Ville, which occupies the most northerly point of the town, and which is sometimes ironically called 'Martledgeville' or 'Snooty Martledge') but no poverty, or at least none worth speaking of. The river still runs near it, although now the wide triangular area of floodplain to the west of the town has been designated a nature reserve; its official title is The Martledge Water Park, but the residents all call it The Meadows. In the centre is a pub called

The Spearman's Boat, flood banks with broad paths at the tops have been built to keep the river in, and the now-dry fields are filled with wild flowers and grass and the sound of summer bees. Dogs are walked there every day, children play, and at night lovers lie within its shadows and find each other. Although the public swimming pool in the centre of Martledge has now closed, there is a large sports centre built on the boundary between the town and the nature reserve, offering exercisers the opportunity to run on the spot whilst looking out over fields and the winding strip of water that originally gave the town its life.

The Suttons still live in Martledge, in the Sutton House, although they have sold much of the land they once owned and the house itself is curtailed. The orchard is still there, the trees mostly wizened and dead, but every year they still fund a family day on the green with food and music and games for the children. They paid for a lych gate and a small wall around the remodelled green in the late nineteenth century and it stands to this day. They are still of the town; the town still owns them.

One of the infant schools has a May Day fair

each year at which the children perform incredibly complex maypole dances, ribbons of all colours twining and twisting in seemingly impossible patterns before the dance is reversed and each of the ribbons freed. The event is always written up in the local weekly paper, the Martledge Gazette and there is always a picture of the children and their teacher – a pretty woman with a kindly face – alongside the article. In the picture everyone is smiling and it always seems to be sunny. There is a park, but the town's four cinemas have all now closed. The library is now a 'Community Hub' but still contains shelf upon shelf of books, and people still borrow them. St Clements is still the grandest church.

There is crime, of course. People drink too much, they fight; behind closed doors men beat women. In the late 1990s, Radovic, Pendlow and Williams, three residents of a bail hostel situated in one of the less pleasant areas of the town, carried out a string of muggings of increasing violence, but were eventually caught and imprisoned. When the Martledge residents realised that they had first met and planned their violence in the hostel, there was a local campaign against it and it was eventually closed, so out of the misery they caused came some good at least. People drive badly on occasion, and they crash; Daisy Coburn was killed when a speeding driver knocked her off her bike, and her mother, it is said, went mad through grief and decorated her bedroom with hundreds of pictures of her dead daughter. Her father campaigned for, and got, sleeping policemen installed on the all the minor roads in the town, which most people publicly thought a good idea but which drivers secretly disliked. In a feast for the Martledge gossips one of the Suttons, James Michael, drove too fast one night along the Baby Way, lost control of his car and hit the side of the Failing Bridge, killing himself and his fiancée, a French girl that no one in the town really knew. People still tie flowers to the repaired railing on the side of the bridge.

Graham Harding, a police constable, was kicked to death outside one of the newer pubs, The Flying Man, by a group of drunken young men fighting each other over football or women or money or some fool thing, and his funeral procession filled the town the week after. There was talk of naming something after the dead officer, but nothing came of it. People steal from shops. People steal from each other. It is a normal town. It has ups, and it has downs. It rains, and it can be cold, but there is warmth here, and love and light against the darkness.

This is Martledge.

This is where Nakata is going to plant ghosts.

~

Nakata had a theory about ghosts.

Of course, Nakata had had a theory about
ghosts for years. It was, he supposed, his stock
in trade, but where before the theories were
things he felt he couldn't trust because they were
so flimsy, this theory felt right, felt like it might
fit and stay fitted, and he thought about it a lot.
On enforced paid sabbatical from his work at the
university, and with no return date yet agreed
because his lawyers, the union and the
university were still fighting over what should be
done with him, and with the cheque from the
Westmorland Hotel's owners still untouched in
his bank account, he had little to do but ponder
what had happened to him over the previous
months and years, and to work out what it
meant, both professionally and personally.

Professionally, he was in a difficult place.
Pilloried in the press, but having discovered that
his reputation wasn't as damaged as he feared,
he had resolved that whatever the outcome of
the current situation, he would not stop his
searching. He had chased ghosts through
underground toilets and along hotel corridors,

and been chased by them across wild headlands past Viking graves, had listened as people told him stories of dead chambermaids and things that stole children from the streets of their home town, and he had wondered. He had studied photographs and films, heard recordings and seen things himself that were hard to explain, and yet only recently had his theory formed and he started to gain anything like a coherent view of these experiences. The problem had always been the *difference*. Each purportedly true ghost story was so different; some were about sound, some about lights or shadows, yet others about shapes. There seemed to be no constancy between them, no link or thread that could allow for a scientific decision or conclusion about what was happening. And the ghosts' abilities also differed from story to story, and sometimes from telling to telling. It made for a confused minefield where few, if any, firm conclusions could be drawn. He needed not simply to prove the existence of ghosts, but to find a unifying thread that could do more than just prove, that could *explain*. The question was, how?

Personally, he was on firmer ground. When Nakata thought about the notion of 'ghosts', he had always thought of something ephemeral, capable in some circumstances of action and reaction yet at other times mindless and repetitive, recordings of the grooves worn into life by the actions of the living. The spirits he had come to accept he believed in despite the scepticism that still lived within him were not things of physical presence, although they could have physical impact, and did not have bodies. They were energy, or energies, little more; capable of exerting themselves on the physical world only in rare circumstances. It meant that Nakata could, for instance, gather the hundreds of under-threat ghosts of a hotel into a bag and feel no weight when he lifted it and see nothing when looked inside it. So far, so simple; the complication was that for other people ghosts seemed to act differently. Amos Wellman, who Nakata had recently worked with on an episode of his television reality show *The Spirit Guider*, seemed to think ghosts had a physical presence of some kind, one that he could touch and grasp and in turn exert force upon. Nakata had seen the man apparently physically force a ghost along its afterlife journey, and had begun to think. If he and Wellman had such different approaches to ghosts and yet both seemed viable, how could this be explained? And what did it mean?

It meant that the ghosts Wellman touched could feel, for one thing; Nakata had heard one scream in pain and fear when Wellman had attacked it, attacked *her*, which meant that Wellman's ghosts had emotions and feelings, were possibly sentient. The ghosts Nakata had hidden in a camera bag to protect them from Wellman had been afraid, that much he knew for sure, meaning they were also sentient, and in that way similar to Wellman's, but still there was the difference between their physical states.

The explanation, which had germinated for Nakata as he walked the corridors of the Westmorland Hotel, had grown and grown in him until now he was sure. Almost sure. It meant, *might* mean, that ghosts were, in part at least, acted upon by their observers and their expectations. Like Schrödinger's Cat, were ghosts in all states until someone glimpsed them, and did the glimpse and the beliefs the observer held then collapsed all those states but one, so that the ghost was then simply a recording, sound or image or movement, solid or insubstantial, an intelligent creature or a mere eternal looping thing?

Did ghosts owe their existence not to the fluttering remains of souls and personalities but instead to the solidities of the living's beliefs?

The more Nakata had thought about it over these last few months, the more he thought that might be true. That ghosts existed he had come to have no doubt, but what kind of existence did they possess, that was the question... that and how he could prove it. Nakata's searches had only ever led him to formless, proofless things, but was that because that was what he expected to find? Some will-o-the-wisp figure in the distance, all wafting curtains and bedsheet trailings, because somewhere inside himself that's what he had decided ghosts were; whereas for Wellman ghosts were things to grapple with, to wrestle into submission, which of course required them to exist on some corporeal plane or other?

It wasn't an entirely original thought, of course; the Owen Group had come to a similar conclusion in the seventies following their Philip experiment, where their entirely created ghost Philip had been able to make noises, rap walls and move tables. It was generally assumed that Philip's physical effects on the world were the result of some kind of group ESP, despite those who claimed that the eerie noises and table-moving were actually the result of another spirit playing with the group. Certainly Owen's wife, in the few emails Nakata had managed to exchange with her before her death in 2009, had believed that that's what the group had managed, but now Nakata wondered. What if, when people died, they left a kind of energy behind that held some essence of its original form, but that could be shaped into new versions of that form by subsequent observation and attention? So that a simple recording of, say, a man walking across a corridor and vanishing into a wall might be given extra abilities, extra routines, even sentience by the simple act of external observation. What if that's what the Owen Group had done, somehow tapped into this energy and formed it into a ghost that could move and interact with them, dimming lights, rattling tables and creating noises? But was Philip real, an actual person being felt and formed by the group, or was the energy mindless and inexorable, like the tide?

Whichever was the case, what did it mean? And how could he prove it? It hurt Nakata's head, filled it with noise because each question led to another question, each answer opening up new lines of enquiry.

Sitting there, just before allowing the website to go live, he sighed. It came down to a single thing, a single point, and that point was a question. There was always a question; an endless series of them in fact, each one a stone in a stream, the answer to each another question just a footfall ahead of him. When he stopped walking, he'd be dead, he supposed, or atrophying in a room somewhere gazing inwards and living in memories as old and dusty as abandoned books in forgotten lofts. His father had never stopped asking, Amy had never stopped asking and never stopped making him ask. Asking and living were two sides of a single thing, two facets of the life he and Amy had started to create before her death. He had lived with ghosts before she had gone, of course, and had buried himself in them afterwards, but only recently had he started to understand, or catch the first glimmers of something that might be understanding.

And now he was in Martledge.

It seemed simple, but like all simple theories its practical application was frustratingly complex. His original plan had been to take people with different opinions as to what ghosts were to haunted places, and record both their responses to the haunting and any physical evidence that might appear, but it soon became clear that proceeding this way would simply create too many variables to keep track of, and would make it impossible to come to any useful, verifiable conclusions. Besides, his recent experiences with taking people into haunted places had not gone well, and he had no real desire to repeat it.

He kept coming back to the Owen Group and Philip. The group, along with the various recreations of the experiment that followed, had come the closest to getting any kind of reputable answer, and finally through their work Nakata thought he might have the shape of something in his mind that might be a solution. Or at least, the first question in a chain that might ultimately lead to one.

Find three stories that had some basis in truth, put them into the public domain, localise them to a specific area, and then see how people react. If anyone reports details or experiences *not* in the stories, see if he can corroborate their experiences with their beliefs or, even better, with historical fact. *There,* he thought, smiling to himself, *simple.*

He had chosen Martledge simply because he had moved there recently and liked it, and it was small and relatively secluded. Researching its history to find the right stories had been time-consuming but oddly relaxing, although building the website had been hugely frustrating. All through the process Nakata thought about Amy, wondering what she'd think of this. Was it a way of wasting time, of avoiding his reconnection with the world about him, losing himself in ghosts again, or would she approve? Would she see it as him reclaiming the thing he had been in danger of losing because of the trial and the publicity after it?

She'd approve, he thought decisively. He glanced at his website again, at the old photos he'd scanned in and the maps he'd used, at the stories and the way he'd placed them in a fairly small area of Martledge so that he could keep a better track of them, and thought again, *She'd approve. She wanted me doing this, wanted me always stepping onto the next stone even if it wobbled underfoot.* He reached out, hand hovering over the keyboard, and had a last moment of anxiety. Did he really want this? Again?

Did he?

Yes. His hand dropped and Nakata loosed his ghosts into the world.

~

The Dancers

One of the wheels had a tilt to it, making it roll unevenly, and it swayed as Minahane pushed it out of the house. It took two hard shoves to get it moving across the rough concrete of the outdoors, and on the second there was a crunch like a breaking bone and the wheel tore loose completely, dropping away and remaining behind them. The damage made Minahane smile.

The loss of the wheel made its movements worse, constantly swerving and dipping as though to escape from him, but Minahane was resolute in his shepherding of it, guiding it across the courtyard created on three sides by the house, barn and back fence. Minahane pushed it until they were past the edge of the barn and in sight of the Lowther house on the other side of the road, by the grassed open space that his children had used as a play area, and in which his now-dead wife had planted borders of herbs that had filled the air with rich, dizzying scents. Minahane stopped then, letting it stop as well. It tilted, settling over because of the missing wheel, and new snow fell and began to cover its top.

Minahane left it where it stood and returned to the barn, opening it in a squeal of rust and damp, swelling wood, and spent several frustrating minutes rooting through piles of old tools and moving rotting bolts of cloth until he found the lump hammer leaning against a wall. Its head was rusted and pitted but still solid, and it was a weight on his shoulder as he walked back out into snow that was falling harder than ever, great fat flakes plunging and swirling around him. It was so heavy now that the air between the flakes was grey and visibility was down to only a hundred feet or so, so that the Lowther house was little more than a blocky shape on the far hillside. The low sun, reduced to a glimmering ball of hazy light, seemed trapped in a prison of branches that reached up from the trees on the far side of the fence. The branches were late-winter bare, clutching around the sun and anchoring themselves to the sullen sky as Minahane hefted the hammer to get a better grip on it and arrived back at the piano.

His first swing took the piano on one of the upright columns that stretched from its feet to the underside of the key bed, snapping it cleanly away and sending it spinning across the ground. The second blow hit the other column but it didn't snap, merely fractured, splinters of wood spraying out as the piano roared in notes from bass to treble.

Minahane took a step back and reset his grip on the hammer, the shaft of it wet with melting snow. The top of the piano was covered now, the flakes settling, the dark wood vanishing as though it was trying to burrow away, to hide. Minahane smiled and hit it again.

This time, the hammer's head chewed into the fallboard that covered the keys, buckling the hinges at one end; it lifted but didn't come loose, and the piano howled, its tortured song shivering the falling snow. It shifted, spinning from the force of the blow, but Minahane wouldn't let it go, wouldn't let it escape and chased it, hitting the broken column again and snapping it in two. Another blow to the fallboard smashed it away, revealing its teeth, and the snow fell heavier and heavier, an inch thick on its top now, and when Minahane hit it again the flakes jumped and slithered.

Another swing split the upper front board in two. Minahane put down the hammer long enough to pull away both parts of broken wood, exposing the pinblock, hammers, rail and strings, and then he had the hammer again and was swinging it directly into the piano's exposed insides. This time the noise it made was a yowl, and Minahane was sure he could hear fear in it as the hammer's head glanced across the taut strings and drew sound from them. Several of the tuning pins popped from the pinboard and the cables whipped out like tentacles, slashing at Minahane who stepped back, then in again, swinging. This time the blow glanced off the hammer rail, slapping across the strings and thumping into the inner side of the case. The wood fractured, exposing dry and pale flesh, and then a final blow broke the case apart and the piano was sagging backwards.

Minahane hit again, the piano swaying and falling so that it was sprawled onto its back, and then he was swinging savagely and repeatedly, feeling the weight of the hammer burning into the muscles of his arms, feeling the snow land on his head and hands and melt in the heat of his anger, the piano screaming and crying, the pinblock first denting then cracking, more strings and pins flailing out, wood chips spraying and dancing, the hammer cycling above his head and down over and over and over, and then it was done.

Minahane couldn't move the metal pinblock, but it didn't matter. Instead, he gathered the wood into a pile, scattering the keys and felt hammers through it as kindling, and set it alight. Old and dry, the wood caught quickly and soon the flames were higher than Minahane, their light haloing, snowflakes falling into them and dying in their embrace. Minahane stood watching until the wood had burned down to little more than a slick of ashes, and then spent a little time pulling the few remaining still-attached strings off the pinboard, coiling each up and putting them in a pile in the barn. The pinblock he struck a few more times for the simple purpose of hearing its dull clang and then, finally, he went back into his house.

Perhaps, now it was dead, they would have some peace.

When the Lowther house burned, the fire birthed in the kitchen.

Afterwards, it was assumed that it started in or near the ancient Aga, reached out to consume the table but found itself blocked from further easy travel by the thick, closed door. Instead, it left the room via the ancient heating ducts that ran between the ground and upper floors, feeding on decades of dust and grease and emerging in the two upper rear rooms of the farmhouse, where carpets and furnishings soon fell to the flames' appetite. Here the doors were open, and the fires left the two rooms, merging into one in the hallway and roaring towards the front bedroom where Ellie Whinfell was sleeping. Ellie, ninety five years old and decaying from the inside from cancer and bitterness, didn't manage to get out of her bed when the flames found her. Rather, her already-wasted flesh puckered and clenched, drawing her up into a boxer's belligerence, the heat baking the screams in her throat, her hair singed and sparked across her scalp and blisters formed, burst and dried to nothing across her skin. By the time Minahane and some of the nearby neighbours had seen the fire and arrived at the house, built by Ellie's ancestors as the family home at the centre of a farm smallholding but now occupied solely by her, Ellie was dead, burned to sticks wrapped in a shroud of ravaged leather.

In the room below where Ellie took her last breaths, the piano stood silent and unharmed.

No one missed Ellie Whinfell. Even whilst sympathetic about her illness, most people agreed she was objectionable, small-minded and petty, and capable of holding a grudge for years until its origins were lost and only the malice and spite remained. Perhaps worse, she was unsociable, refusing to allow people into her home and never joining in the activities that bonded the rest of Martledge together. Instead, she remained indoors, emerging only to shop or to pay the labourers that tended her land and cattle. At night, passers-by would hear her playing the piano and those who passed close enough swore that sometimes they could hear feet banging on the floor as though she was dancing, although no one could imagine such movement from that sour, joyless woman. The tunes she played were often heard long into the night's smallest hours, the notes sometimes fading only as the sun rose, although no one mentioned it; some time in the past it had been suggested to her that playing an instrument so early in the morning might disturb her neighbours, and the suggester had been sent away with vitriol and scorn poured in their ears. Ellie Whinfell, it was agreed, was a woman of little warmth and much anger.

Minahane heard the piano on the evenings when the wind was right and the air clear, and despite how he felt about Ellie, he liked the sound of it; Ellie played tunes that were sometimes slow and mournful, other times bombastic and loud, still others delicate and achingly beautiful, and when they floated into Minahane's home they sounded as though they were coming from the very earth that surrounded him.

The fire in Ellie's home destroyed most of the building except the front ground floor rooms, its roof burned away and fallen in so that it looked like an ancient ruin rather than a recently inhabited home. Rain harried the damaged structure further, smearing ash down the few unbroken windows and creating torrents that spilled from buckled gutters and slathered across the brickwork. No relatives came to fix the property, although there were distant cousins to whom ownership passed; instead a local lawyer auctioned what few possessions were salvageable from the undamaged rooms, and what couldn't be sold he gave away. It was from him that Minahane got the piano, buying it on impulse because of the memory of those tunes, and with some half-formed plan in his head of filling his evenings with learning so that he might one day produce something so beautiful. He was lonely now that Meg had walked the coffin path and the children had moved away, and he thought the piano might fill the opening gaps in his life.

Minahane got three local labourers to help him move the piano, which smelled of smoke and fire when they took it from the Lowther house. Minahane imagined he could see wisps of black soot blow free from the instrument as they carried it across the road and into his house through a stiffening breeze, cleaning it, making it fresh and new. He had cleared a space for the piano in his parlour, pushing back the now-unused dining table, and he had the men set it against the wall. It looked good, he decided, and made the room seem more elegant somehow. He wished they had thought to do this when Meg was alive, and was overtaken by a sudden wave of sadness that he had never even thought about setting Meg to music, or setting music in front of Meg. She had been the creative one out of the two of them, and he was sure she'd have mastered the piano with ease and made wondrous things flow from it.

His own first touch of the keyboard, after he was sure the men were gone and out of earshot, produced a sound that wasn't exactly displeasing but that jarred, was discordant and contained only the most distant echoes of the things Ellie had teased from it. His fingers looked graceless and thick perched above the keys, unable to achieve the dexterity he felt he would need to stretch to make chords, to bring in the minor black notes as well as the major ivory ones. He had bought himself a book of piano basics, but looking at it now the diagrams made little sense and he eventually closed it, disheartened, and went to bed.

That night the piano woke Minahane.

It was only a few notes, so soft that they might almost have been part of a dream. Minahane rolled over and opened his eyes and listened, but no more sound came. Perhaps the instrument was simply settling, adjusting itself to its new home, he thought, the wood causing the hammers to strike the strings. It didn't matter, not really; if anything, the notes were comforting, as gentle as the last sleepy whisper of a lover in his ear as he drifted back off.

The next night there were more notes from the darkness of the room below, louder, and the night after more again.

That third time Minahane rose and padded downstairs, the chill night air puckering his skin into marbled plains of prickle and hair. He slept naked and his scrotum drew up against itself as he descended the stairs, shrivelling to a ridged cup between his legs. The notes carried on as he approached, not fading as they had the previous nights, jagged single and double strikes creating a flat tune in the air that had no melody and no pattern. When Minahane opened the door into the parlour, however, the noises stopped. The piano's lid (*Fallboard*, he thought, *it's a fallboard*) was down, the keyboard covered, and when he touched it, it was cold. He wondered if mice had somehow got inside the instrument and were playing around on its strings, but when he opened the upper front board and peered inside, he could see nothing except the instrument's bones and muscles. Experimentally, he sat and lifted the fallboard, smiling at the image of himself naked in front of the piano, and then played a few notes. They were soft, and no matter how hard he struck the keys he couldn't make them sound as loud as the ones he had heard a few moments ago.

Was the instrument still settling? Or expanding or contracting because his home was damper or dryer or warmer or colder than Ellie's had been? He didn't know, but supposed that must be it. He knew little about instruments and music beyond the listening of it, and had no idea what to expect of instruments in the home. Were they susceptible to drafts and chills? Did their position in the room matter? Returning to his empty bed, Minahane resolved to find out, and to redouble his efforts to learn to play the piano.

He found a girl in Upper Wells who was happy to visit him weekly, and she began to teach him the rudiments. Minahane discovered, gratified, that his fingers soon learned the positions they needed to be in and that he could coax simple tunes from the piano, although they sounded terribly blocky and stolid compared to the notes that had drifted to his ears from Ellie's house. He found that he quite enjoyed the monotony of practice in the evenings, losing himself to repetition and reiteration, but still within that hearing slight changes and improvements to what he was producing. Other than when he caressed its keys, the piano remained silent.

The dancers came just after Christmas.

The festive season was always hard for Minahane. The weather tended to close in around Martledge, isolating it in a bubble of its own light, surrounded by the oppressive absence of Meg and the pressure of the duty-invitations his children sent him to spend the season with them. As the holidays approached the weight of it all stopped him from enjoying the piano, stopped him from enjoying food, stopped him sleeping and finally almost stopped his breathing. Not without a sense of grudging, loving bullying, Minahane eventually relented and agreed to the trip out of Martledge, finding during his time away that his children appeared to genuinely want him with them and that the world seemed both larger yet, oddly, less spacious away from the place he called home. During the week he played no piano and missed it, feeling his fingers stiffen, losing some of their recently learned flexibility.

He returned home late in the evening in one of the last days of the year after a day of travel and branch line changes and godawful food, handed over counters in greaseproof paper wrappings, and he was tired. He dropped his bags in the hallway of the house, shut the door behind him, muttered, "Hang spring cleaning," and went straight up to his bedroom, where his bed welcomed with open, familiar arms.

He heard the feet in the night's darkest space. They drew him from sleep with a start, the sound of steps clattering across his parlour floor, the sound of the creaking boards as familiar to him as the beat of his own heart. Feet, more than one set, perhaps three, moving around his room.

Burglars? It seemed unlikely, but possible. Minahane got out of bed, took the time to pull on trousers and an undershirt, and then crept down the stairs. He walked without thinking, feet going to the steps and spaces where the boards beneath him wouldn't react to his weight, knowing how to move silently along the short arteries of his home. He came to the parlour door, placed his head against it and listened. There a sharp bang and the piano strings echoed, as though someone had raised the lid and dropped it. Another bang and this time a series of single note jabs, a staccato burst like Morse code signals from a long-forgotten war. Minahane reached for the door handle, still unsure what he was listening to in the room beyond, when the footsteps started again. There was a rhythm to them now, a tapping beat, stuttering but present.

And then the piano howled.

Minahane pushed open the door without thinking, expecting to see...what? Drunk people playing on his piano and dancing around the room, a broken window their entry point? Instead, there were shadows and the dim shapes of his furniture but nothing else; no burglars, although for a moment the shades gathering at the corners of the room seemed to recede and move, hunching down, vanishing. They were people but not people, like shadows that had escaped their owners slouching down against his walls to hide.

The piano was along against the wall. Its fallboard was up and its keys showing, toothsome like the grin of a shark.

The next morning, dressed but not rested, Minahane returned to the parlour and the piano. Caught by the weak sun arching in through the windows, the piano was beautiful, its dark wood lustrous and the keys gleaming. Minahane sat on the stool in front of it, placed his fingers on the keys and started to pick out scales. As he played, he thought. Had he really heard anything last night? He drifted slightly, imagining his first idea made ridiculous, that a group of men wearing dark trousers and striped jumpers and masks had broken in, that they had put down their hessian sacks (marked, of course, 'Swag') and gathered around the piano, that one had started to play while the others danced, somehow darting to the corners and avoiding his gaze as he opened the door. Nonsense, but it didn't make him smile because he had heard something, he *had*. Several somethings, overlapping, competing for space in his hearing, not the dulcimer tones of madness or dementia but *something*. A piano, and steps, feet, movement.

Besides, there was the piano. The piano. Minahane looked down at the instrument's keys, remembering nights of noise and notes, remembering it grinning at him in the dark last night and another image swirled in his head, one of people caught by the wrists by cruelly tight turns of wire that tethered them to the piano, dragging them with it wherever it went. And would they dance, these captives, would they dance when the piano played and the tunes reached out into the morning darkness? Yes, thought Minahane, yes they would otherwise the knots would turn and tighten, dig in further, wrenching joints and tearing dead skin.

Minahane snatched his hands away from the keys, suddenly terrified. The dancers he had heard were not people but something less, the dead; he knew it, captives of the thing in front of him, knew it from its ferocious grin and from the way that the keys seemed to rise with his fingers, to lift off the keybed further than they had any right to be able to reach and to try to remain adhered to his skin, to keep him close. He stood, stepping back and knocking over the stool. Was that it? Did the piano drag with it the people who had played it, make them dance around it?

No. It was madness.

Yes, because he *knew*. Minahane took another step back and the fallboard snapped down, resonating the strings of the instrument in an atonal murmur. Then, as he watched, the fallboard banged back up and the keys grinned at him, awaiting his touch.

"No," he whispered, then said aloud, "No." The fallboard clattered shut then opened again, the lips of some great beast flapping its appetite. Minahane backed out of the room, half expecting the piano to start rolling towards him but it remained motionless, simply banging the lid up and down, up and down, harder and faster, until the sounds emanating from the thing were a single mass of noise, almost physical in its weight, that followed him as he fled up the stairs and to his room.

Minahane's first thought was to run, and he'd got as far as pulling his still packed bag onto the bed, cramming fresh clothes into it, before he stopped. Where would he go? Back to one of his children's homes? To a neighbour? And say what, that a piano was playing itself and torturing the souls, or ghosts, or spirits of its previous players every night? That it had rested when it first arrived with him but now was back to full strength and was starting to build up its cruelties again? They'd think him mad, driven there by grief and loneliness, just a silly old man living by himself with only the ghosts in his head for company, another of Martledge's lost folk, and he wasn't that, wasn't at all because this was real, was actual. Was terrible.

Minahane sat on the bed, breathed out, tried to think, and that was when the tune floated up the stairs.

It was one of the ones he had played as a learning piece, a simple thing called 'The Grasshopper' that used the right hand to play a basic six note melody and the left to underpin it with a deeper three note floor. When Minahane played it it sounded choppy and uneven, but here it was as it was meant to be, flowing perfectly, the notes smoothing into each other as though their edges were melted together to form a sonorous whole, rather the forced-together separates that Minahane created. He listened, recognising beauty in what he was hearing even as he realised what it meant.

The piano was playing itself.

Before he went down, Minahane made sure his clothes were straight and tidy so that he could present his best possible self, hiding his fear and confusion behind a straight tie, buttoned weskit and neatly pressed trousers. Descending the stairs he passed a window through which he saw the Lowther house and it made him think of Ellie Whinfell, so long thought of as a bitter crone, but had they all been wrong? As 'The Grasshopper' began again below him, Minahane wondered if maybe she had not been a recluse by choice, but rather trapped in her home by the piano and the impossible music and the sound of dancing? Because who, really, could she have told, and what could she have done?

At the parlour door, Minahane paused, listening. Despite everything, the simple tune drifting through the door was beautiful, played so well that it was almost beyond music, had become something alive and ethereal. Finally, knowing he had no choice, that if he didn't act he'd spend the rest of his life replaying this moment and regretting it and cursing his cowardice, he opened the door.

This time, the music didn't stop, and Minahane saw the dancers.

There were three of them, dark shapes in the sunlight moving in a stately rhythm around the room. They were unclear around their edges as though blurring away into the daylight, had no limbs or features, no faces, were simply masses that moved like people under shrouds while the piano played on. Its keys were not moving but the tune emerged from it still, coming to an end as Minahane stepped over the threshold. Instead of starting again, however, the piano fell silent. Its fallboard, although already up, seemed to push back further, exposing the piano's teeth. It grinned at him, inviting him to come and play it. He sensed, rather than saw, the dancers watch him expectantly, and went to the piano. Although he had not picked it up, the stool was back upright in front of it, angled out so that he could sit without effort, pulling himself in close after. He reached out, not wanting to touch the instrument but knowing now what it wanted. Its grin seemed to get wider as his fingers came closer, anticipating, and then they were on the ivory and feeling the cool tingle of it against his skin, and he felt the music ripple through him.

Minahane started to play.

He started with 'The Grasshopper', played it better than he had ever played it before, feeling the notes emerge from under his touch in ways that he had never experienced before, and when the tune was over he started playing something else from his 'Learn to Play' book. He didn't have the book in front of him, but he played from memory and played well, played *perfectly*, and when that one was done he played another and then another and then Minahane started to play things that he had never heard or played before.

And the dancers danced.

They still became no clearer, remained dark and shifting shapes in the weak indoor winter light, moving around each other in careful curves, things that might have been shoulders dropping and rising, shapes that might be heads bobbing. Minahane's fingers moved faster across the keys, teasing more and more elegance from them, and as his playing created more and more complex structures the dances became more complex alongside them. The three figures were spinning and weaving around each other now in intricate steps, behind and in front of each other, sometimes moving alongside each other in a row and other times in swirling patterns, starting to increase in speed and his fingers ached but still he played and the piano grinned and grinned and the tunes went on and on.

How long they were in the parlour together he didn't know. Hours and hours though, far into the night he played, until the sweat that trickled down his body had soaked through his clothes and left him feeling clammy and cold, until his fingers were raw, the tips of them red and peeling, the joints past aching, painful now, swelling with effort. The keys were warm and glistening with drops of perspiration and tiny smears of blood when he finally finished, when the piano let him stop. Sitting, exhausted, he watched as the sweat and blood soaked into the keys and disappeared.

The dancers never stopped moving, never became any clearer over the course of the tunes he played although Minahane came to think he could make out differences between them. One seemed taller, moved like a man, the other two were shorter and gave the impression of being female. It was something in the way they moved and the shapes their edges created and then lost, he thought, some sense of femininity and masculinity, of them having individual identities, and God help him and God help her, he thought one might be Ellie Whinfell. She had been hunched and thin at the end, and the shadow was hunched and thin as well, and it danced with a cancered jerk and shift that made him think of how she had walked when she left her home. He watched as he played, mesmerised and terrified and tired, and when he stopped the dancers fell apart like wet paper shapes in swirling water.

Despite it all, Minahane slept when he got himself into his bed, going somewhere dark and dreamless and waking late the next morning. His hands ached terribly, had swollen so that moving hurt, so he lay still and tried to think. Was this what Ellie had had to put up with all those years, being forced to play the piano at night, feeding it with her time and sweat and attention? With her blood? Creating tunes for dancers when alive, now tethered in some way to the piano and made to dance herself after her death?

And were the other two dancers earlier players of the piano, also tethered somehow?

Was he now tethered to it?

That got Minahane moving and he rose, cradling his hands against himself, and dressed slowly. It hurt to pull his shirt on and to do the buttons and he couldn't face pulling on socks so he went barefoot, going down to the parlour and opening the door before his resolution failed him. The piano was where it had been the previous night, where it always been, against the wall. It looked bloated, as though it had fed well. He supposed it had, on him. Its fallboard was down, covering the keys. Was it asleep? Did it sleep?

Minahane sat and touched the wood of the top board. It was warm, felt alive somehow, more than just wood. He tapped it, gently, not wanting to wake it. Even now he could feel a tug in his stomach and wrists. Despite the pain, despite the fear, he wanted to open it and let his fingers sit on the keys, let the notes come forth, listen as they formed into tunes and rhythms and melodies, wanted to feel his blistered fingers against the cool ivory. Before he realised what he was doing, his hands were on the fallboard, and he jumped back from the instrument. "What are you?" he asked aloud, but the piano did nothing, simply slept.

The dancers didn't come that night or the next day. Minahane didn't leave his house and didn't go into the parlour, instead trying to act normally. He cleaned and cooked, feeling the movement come slowly back into his fingers as the pain and swelling started to recede, watching as pads of new skin formed on their tips, and tried to think about what to do. The piano had taken up residence in his parlour, had been invited in by him, and now he had to deal with it. He deliberately didn't go back into the parlour, and did not look at the piano again.

He felt its pull, though, constant, trying to draw him back to it so that he would play, a fishline tension that pulled and dug at him. Was this how Ellie had felt, all those years? Every day waiting for the night and the time to play, every night letting the music loose and watching the dancers spin and turn around her? Her life marked out by tune and litany, by the grinning teeth of the piano and the pressures it placed upon her? Isolated and lost, never allowing anyone in her home or her life for fear they'd think her mad, as Minahane thought they would him if he spoke about this, or for fear that the piano would ensnare them too?

Rather than shunning the community she had lived in, had she actually been protecting it? Had she lived in that house, alone and bullied, for all those years while her neighbours treated her like a pariah the few times she went out? Minahane felt a wave of sadness and anger, at himself as much as at the piano, for the things that Ellie and the two other dancers had experienced, for all the misery and terror that they had endured and were enduring still. How many times had he dismissed Ellie as a sour spinster, ignoring her in the street, never going to her and asking if she needed help?

And was that to be his fate now? An old man, lonely and becoming an outcast in the village he had lived in all his life, watching ghosts waltz as he wasted away?

No. For whatever reason Ellie and the earlier players, if that's what the other two dancers were, hadn't been able to act or free themselves; it wasn't going to happen to him.

As dusk fell on the second night there was a bang from the parlour and a throaty sounding of notes. The fallboard, Minahane suspected, had just yawned open. The piano was awake again, and maybe the dancers were already waiting. Instead of going to it, however, Minahane began to walk around his home, ignoring the call of it, ignoring the draw of it, determined not to give in. Notes jagged out of the parlour, harsh and insistent, and he started to hum to cover them, clenching and unclenching his fists, letting the pain that remained in them bite through the piano's call. He muttered and hummed to himself, drowning it.

Minahane walked throughout the night, and the piano played its increasingly angry song to summon him, and he thought of Meg and his children and the place he hoped to go after he died and how it was not a place where he would want to dance, and in the morning as the sun crept into the sky and as the snow began to fall he thought about the lump hammer, and he thought about fire.

The day after he killed the piano, Minahane heard the ghost of notes from outside the house.

Looking out, he saw three dark shapes standing around the lump in the snow where the remains of the piano lay. A zephyr of wind spun across it, lifting flakes and ash and for a moment it formed a black spiral that turned and spun and that caught at the edges of the figures and drew them into itself and then they were gone, vanished away to nothing. Ellie Whinfell, if that's who it really was, raised what might have been a hand to him before she disappeared.

The dancers were free. Minhane sat on the piano stool and, much to his surprise, started to cry. As he did so his fingers moved, searching for keys to play.

~

Nakata was that desperate to read the comments on the website, his palms itched, but he wouldn't let himself look.

It was a decision he'd come to moments after making the website live, because he was suddenly struck by the notion that if he read the comments he risked absorbing the information and being influenced, and anything he then saw or heard, any conclusions he came to as a result of those experiences, could and would be subject to additional questioning. At best he would be accused of confirmation bias; at worst, direct influence or even fraud. That he was not conducting a 'perfect' experiment already opened him up to criticism and critical dismissal, he knew, but he wanted to retain some semblance of scientific rigour, even if it was limited. He was not being peer reviewed, there was no board oversight and no panel was helping to develop the experiment. This was for him; him and the dead.

So, rather than look, Nakata steeled himself and did not visit either the website or its control panel, doing nothing other than noting emails informing him of comments when they arrived in his inbox. He had set up a new email to handle this specific project, so avoiding reading them was relatively easy; he simply didn't open the inbox and look at what was inside. He knew from his phone notifications, though, that people were responding to each of the stories, adding comments. Were they dismissing them? Discussing them?

Adding to them?

Part of the problem was that Nakata, although relatively new as a Martledge resident, was known; not famous, certainly, but with a certain reputation. He'd been in the papers, mostly in a negative light, and had recently been called 'Ghost Man' and 'Ghost Hunter' – neither of which was entirely true – and once 'The Ghost Idiot', which was maybe more accurate. He didn't want his neighbours talking to him about ghosts, these or any others, which meant that, as far as possible, he had to stay indoors. He had to hit the end of this thing – not quite an experiment, but something more than a casual hobby – as neutrally as possible, so that he could see if what happened fitted his theory, or if his theory fitted what happened. He had to try to see whether or not people would make ghosts in their own images. Would they change the ghosts he made, and if so how?

Would *he* be able to see the ghosts *they* made?

To try to keep some level of anonymity Nakata had gone to some lengths to make sure that the website couldn't be traced back to him, so that all the developing information about these three of Martledge's ghosts, or whatever they were, would only come through the site itself. There were, he thought, additional papers he might do on how things developed if there was only this single source of information. If the press reported on the ghosts, for example, how would they do so? And could he track their trails, like a big game hunter pursuing prey through the grasslands or the jungle? He didn't know, but it would be interesting to try – fun, even.

Nakata got his patience from his father, although it manifested in different ways. Nakata's patience was one of intent, directed at a purpose. He could sit in silence, motionless, listen for sounds that should not be there for hours at a stretch, could concentrate on gauges and dials whilst recording minute changes for as long as it took. Patience as a tool to achieve a purpose. His father, though, who had been the calmest man Nakata had ever known, had patience like a stone in the desert. He had endured a lifetime of petty – and not so petty – racism, had struggled for acceptance and to make his way, and had ended up at a point where he rushed nothing and strained against little. At times like this Nakata wondered what his dad would have done. Read a book, probably, or cooked, his two favourite pastimes. Decided on a course of action and then smilingly stuck to it, not worrying. He and Nakata's mother had died close to each other, both too young, and Nakata had been carrying their ghosts not in a bag but inside himself ever since. *If I'm right,* he thought, *then my focus has changed them*, and that made him oddly uneasy, as though he was creating something new and in the process somehow betraying them, and wondered what they'd have said if he'd tried to explain all this to them. His mum would have laughed. His dad would have just smiled and said, "You can't do anything about it, so don't let it bother you," and Nakata wished he could see them again and hug them. He missed them both. His father had once said, "All I need is you and your mum and the space inside our home, Richard, that's all I'll ever need." and Nakata had always envied him that contentment, it was where he and his father had differed. Nakata closed his eyes and allowed himself to think not of ghosts but of his parents, and of the things they had given him.

Nakata smiled, remembering, and the itch in his hands faded.

~

The Smiling Man

"It won't do, van Hewson, it won't do at all."

The chair of the local Board of Health peered at the sexton over the glittering lowers of his half-moon spectacles and tapped the report on the table in front of him for emphasis. "St Clements' graveyard is full, you admit it yourself?"

"Yes," replied van Hewson, agreeably enough. There was little point in denying what the Ratepayers Association's report said.

"There is, I am told, scarcely inches between burial plots and barely two feet of earth between the air and the faces of the dead, or at least, the tops of their coffins?"

"Yes" again because really, what was the point in denying it? The other board members variously shook their heads or mumbled in disapproval. Beside van Hewson, the Reverend Booth shifted uncomfortably.

"And when new burials are required? What do you do?" asked the chair, a small, round fellow called Bassett, whose hangdog face resembled the dog he was presumably named after. His jowls were edged by a fearsome pair of mutton chops and the cord of his glasses kept tangling in the wiry hair in front of his ears and needed pulling free.

"Well, what can we do?" asked Booth, a touch of plaintiveness creeping in to his voice. Van Hewson tried to not to let his irritation show as Booth carried on.

"The graveyard has been extended three times, but the last request for an extension was refused by the Parish. Our burial records go back to 1762 but there are gravestones with dates as far back as 1590, so we know that there are more dead than we have numbers for. We have no space but the dead keep knocking on our doors. The crypts under the church are full, the bones of the dead are packed four or five deep in some places, and when the parishioners kneel Sunday after Sunday to pray, they do so in the dust of their ancestors."

"And we sympathise," Bassett said, "but there can be no more burials in the ground, except for those that can go in family plots with at least five feet of earth between coffin and air, or where you have made space. The Home Office has already agreed to a review of the situation in light of public health concerns, and when that review is concluded I'm sure an effective long term solution will be found, but until then find a way, gentlemen, to prevent the current closeness of the dead to the living."

"But the dead are *always* close to the living in God," said Booth, quite spoiling the oratorical flow he had built up in his earlier, surprisingly accurate and impassioned comment. Besides, thought van Hewson, the board didn't know the half of it; if they had done, they'd have been far more worried.

Everyone knew that the St Clements's graveyard was full, of course. Every time it rained the surface of the path washed away to reveal jawbones and finger bones and once, the dome of a skull, although who the brainpan had once belonged to was never ascertained. In particularly heavy storms the bones themselves would escape the earth and wash down the paths and be found scattered through Martledge's streets, and these were always gathered and cast into a midden grave beyond the rear of the churchyard; although it was technically in unconsecrated ground Booth always blessed the offerings as they were covered in their thin scrub of soil.

Following the instruction from the Health Board, the first thing they did was hire a pair of local labourers to remove all the old, unreadable gravestones, to smash them and to use the rubble to line a bigger midden grave dug specially for the purpose next to the existing one. That gave the churchyard an appearance of greater space, which pleased most people, and the fact that van Hewson had instructed the men to leave any newer stone also meant that no one living complained about barbarous treatment of their dead relatives.

The next stage was to dig new graves earlier than usual, before dawn by the light of lanterns, and to remove any coffin remnants and bones that appeared in the dig at an inconveniently shallow depth. These were buried under the church floor below the congregation's unsuspecting feet, or in the midden if the remains had rotted down enough, the labourers paid for the silence as well as their muscle. It meant that the church could still carry out burials, take the interment fee, and if rains washed away topsoil from the paths in the churchyards to reveal pale glimmers of old bone, silver buckles and buttons, occasional leather edges or strips of material, then that was surely a small price to pay. "We are," said Booth to van Hewson while in one of his ruminative moods, "a church built on the dead. It is our tradition, and our burden." Everyone was used to it, and it had been this way for years, and no one would really have bothered except for the pokings of a nosy assessor who had raised the issue with the Ratepayer's Association, who had raised it with the Health Board who had, in turn, raised it with the Home Office whilst also handing the issue's responsibility lock stock and barrel back to Booth and his sexton.

George Dent had been buried in the churchyard only twenty years previously, and although he had no family he had a hefty, solid gravestone that he had left provision for in his will. The engraving on the stone simply gave the dates of Dent's life and death and said below, *He sleeps in solitary depths*. Dent's grave had been put at the back of the consecrated ground, near the wall, as it was popularly and correctly assumed that few people would visit the grave after the service. Over the intervening years the stone weathered, moss growing in the grooves of the chiselled lettering and obscuring them, but in truth no one minded because George Dent hadn't been popular in Martledge. It wasn't that he was a miser or a curmudgeon; he gave regularly to church funds and would join in the various events on the green, including the yearly pace-egging celebration during which he cheered on the children dressed as The Bold Slasher, the Black Morocco King and the Devil and gave generously to the Tosspot, a boy dressed in girl's clothing carrying a bucket for donations. He was quiet and worked hard at the gunpowder works outside Martledge as their chief accountant, and was always dressed correctly but never ostentatiously. No, Dent's lack of popularity was because he *looked*.

Dent looked at the girls before they came to their menses, when they were flat and skinny like saplings, he looked at their sisters when their breasts were in bud like spring flowers, he looked at their mothers and their aunts when they were in full bloom and his eyes were on their faces but also somehow crawling over their skin and taking delight in the way it made the looked-upon feel, and everyone knew Dent delighted in this because when he looked, he smiled. It was a half-smile, always, a curl to the lips as though he knew something that no one else did, had a secret that he might share if only he was asked the right way. When Dent looked at the Martledge girls and women and smiled, they felt unclean, as though he had touched them in private places with secret fingers.

Dent's remains were moved one rainy night as more bone fragments were harried free from the swollen ground and carried out into Martledge. Booth ordered his body removed from his allotted grave and reburied on the far side of the church wall, in the common unconsecrated ground but away from the middens, while the bodies that had been buried over the years on top of Dent's were dropped into the middens and cursorily blessed. His stone was left where it stood, for appearances' sake and because the man had left a bequest to the church and deserved to be shown some respect. That had been in early spring, nearly two months after the Health Board meeting. The trouble didn't start until a few weeks later.

Florence Holt was late. Not so late that Pa would be furious but late enough that he'd be stern, and stern was the road to furious if the situation wasn't handled right, so she walked fast. Not too fast, though, because she didn't want to be flustered when she arrived home, because flustered might make Pa think about what her and Peter had been doing, and if he came to the right conclusion about that then everything would deteriorate from there. Instead, she walked fast, making sure her clothes didn't get messy, keeping her cape around her to keep the worst of the rain out. She'd pinned her hair back up under her cap before she'd left, thank God, and the rain had only just started so she wasn't too messy. She would, she thought, get away with it.

It was only a few minutes to home now; she simply had to cross the green and then walk several streets back to the tiny terrace she shared with Pa and the others, her sisters and brothers.

Until recently, Ma had been there too, always ready to smile when she came in, always putting herself between Florence and Pa, but now she was gone and Florence's world seemed much smaller. Martledge seemed smaller, hemming her in, pressing down on her, and she hoped that Peter would expand her world's horizons again, take her away from it all to somewhere she could call her own.

Through the lych gate now, the Sutton Gate she supposed she should think of it as, its arched passage dark and echoing, only a few steps away now, and then someone stepped out from the shadows at the side of the gate as she emerged into the green and drew a cold finger across the back of her neck.

Florence started, turned, but there was no one there, just an impression of someone slipping through the rain around the gate to disappear along its side. "Hello," she called, hurrying to the corner and looking along the outer wall of the lych gate. The side of the structure was deserted.

"Peter?" she called, but not too loudly. She didn't want anyone in the nearby houses to hear her. Glancing over, she saw that both pubs' lights were still on, which increased the chance of being seen by drinkers leaving either establishment. "Peter," she said again, this time hissing it so that he might hear how little she was amused. The rain pattered against her cap and shoulders, drizzling down her cape and dripping to the ground below. No reply.

"Peter," one last time, kinder now in case he had wanted simply a last kiss, but still nothing. She turned again, and the man standing immediately behind her reached up and trailed his fingers across her cheek. Florence screamed and the man darted away, merging with the shadows on the far side of the green.

Everyone thought it was Lewis Guthrie who had attacked Florence, although 'attacked' was probably too strong a word for it, and the Reverend Booth went to visit Guthrie and his mother and gave the man a stern talking too. Guthrie wept and howled during the reverend's visit, claiming he had not left the house all night, and his mother confirmed this, but what could you expect of a simpleton and his mother? Booth said his piece and left, and the next day he and van Hewson decided on the last set of graves to dig up while labourers collected the bone fragments, including a jawbone with teeth still attached, that now littered the roads around the church and green. They had bought themselves a few months' more burials, he supposed, but probably not much more. Every little helped.

Alice Moreby woke because someone had spoken. What had they said? Nothing complicated, she knew, and now there was silence. A single word, perhaps two at most. She rolled over in her bed and looked at the ceiling, trying to listen. Was one of the children awake? Kayleigh fretted at night in the rain, not liking the sound it made against the window of her room, and Samuel was teething, but no, neither child was audible. Had Joe spoken in his sleep? He'd done it before, a half-formed broth of words and sound in which phrases could sometimes be made out, but he slept next to her breathing slow and easy. Then what? Someone in the street?

"Hello, Alice," said a voice. Alice tried to scream and couldn't. Fear had her by the throat, was squeezing just enough to prevent words forming, was turning her head towards the window from where the sound had come. *Joe*, she wanted to cry, *Joe*, but nothing would emerge. The voice spoke again, a single foul word as she rose from the bed, and now there was a kind of sullen anger mixing with the fear, driving her on because this was her home, her bedroom, and she would not be frightened in her own bedroom, the sanctuary in her house. Her hands came up as she reached the window, taking hold of the drapes' edges as the voice said her name a last time, low and silvery and somehow wet and rank. Breath heaving in and out of her chest, her body shaking and still unable to speak, Alice pulled apart the curtains.

George Dent smiled at her. Alice and Joe's bedroom was on the upper floor of the house yet Dent appeared to be holding on to nothing, just hanging in the air smiling that slow half smile, and then dropped away, vanishing into the night as Alice Moreby found her voice and managed, at last, to scream Joe's name.

It went on.

Grace Cole was walking back along the top of the floodwall by the river one dusktime a week or so later, the river to one side below her and the fields below her to the other; the sounds of tiny flies darting hither and yon and the flop and spit of the river's surface breaking as fish went after the flies her companion on her walk. She had been delivering new cloths and curtains made by her mother to the landlord at The Spearman's Boat and had stayed to help the landlord's wife, the sweet, simple Elise, hang them. They made the dining area seem much brighter, Grace thought, and liked the way her mother's delicate weaving had helped the Spearman (as everyone in Martledge called it) seem a better place. The bargees no longer travelled the river in the numbers they once had, so the Spearman was setting itself as a gentleman's rest on the journey between towns, and was hoping to host cattle and farm auctions soon. Her mother's mark in the dining area was helping the Spearman on its way.

As she walked, enjoying the day's transition into night and the warmth of the air, Grace heard something behind her. She turned, looking first at the river in case something had broken the water; there were eels here, and rats that the labourers would bring ratting dogs to catch on sunny days, but nothing appeared to have disturbed the water's surface except for the tiny flies and the less-tiny fish below. The other way was the fields, and they seemed empty. At the base of the flood bank was a thick fringe of high, waving grass that gave way to the fields after a few feet, the grass higher than a man at this time of the year.

Someone was in the fringe.

Grace couldn't see them, but she could see the trail they were creating as a kind of ruffle in the grass's surface, a narrow strip of stems bending and swaying in patterns different from the rest of the grass's wind movement. The nearest end of the trail was perhaps twenty feet back from her and she watched as it crept closer. There was something stealthy about the way she could see the trail but not its creator, as though they were crouching low and trying to remain unseen. The hair on her arms prickled, her scalp tightening slightly. She debating calling out, even opened her mouth, and then the trail stopped moving.

Even though Grace could not see anyone in the grass, which was dark like the sea at night, she felt she was being watched by whoever was in the shadows below her. She started walking again, slowly, looking back over her shoulder as she did so, and there was a face peering at her from the top of the grass.

It was insipid, the face, the eyes featureless below an expanse of forehead the colour of old whey; the nose was long and thin and the mouth below it was smiling a little half smile and Grace screamed because two hands were rising out of the grass in front of the face, the arms bare, and the figure was rising behind the hands, naked and pale as it leapt up and then she was running.

Grace ran along the top of the flood bank listening to the sound of the grass thrashing from behind and was it getting closer, yes, it was, closer and closer and her breath was ragged in her throat now, knives scouring the inside of her chest every time she inhaled.

She risked a look over her shoulder, saw something pinkish white arrowing through the fringe of grass, still behind her but gaining, and then she was angling down the side of the bank and into the high grass herself, feeling it slap and scratch at her, hearing the dull thud of her pursuer's feet hitting the earth but not their breathing, no words, and then Grace was out of the grass and onto the path that curved away from the river and would lead her back to

Martledge. She looked around again, kicking her legs out so that they wouldn't tangle in her skirts and bring her down, and the pale pink thing was running almost out of the grass now, close behind her, almost close enough to reach out and touch and she wanted to scream but needed all the air she had for her flight and the man, because it was a man, was looking at her as they ran and smiling, smiling a secret little smile as the grass striped his naked chest and legs.

Grace tried to run faster but there was no more left in her, and as the path cut away from the river and started back to the town between two of the fields, she knew that her time had come; the man behind her would pounce any second and that would be her done and gone. She didn't give up, though, she ran and ran until her vision was spotting black as though she had blood in her eyes, until her belly was clenching and spasming like a knotting thing, until her throat burned with pain and nausea, and her arms ached from pumping and grasping at air to try to keep pulling herself forwards and then she tripped and was falling.

Grace hit the ground hard, jolting her head against the earth and making her teeth click together. Her hands immediately started burning where they had scraped through the dirt, and she waited for the man to land on her back.

It didn't happen. Eventually, feeling sick, feeling so frightened that her heart seemed to be bolting loose inside her, Grace had little choice but to roll over and sit up. She looked back down the path and saw the man, now little more than a pink and ivory blur, still standing in the grass at the base of the flood bank. Grace stood, keeping the man in her sight whilst trying to glance around for a rock or something else to throw at him if he approached her. There was nothing, but it didn't matter because the man, instead of following, faded back into the shadows behind him.

Grace looked down at her dirty dress, at her scratched and punctured hands, remembered the smile on the man's face, and started to cry.

Three nights later, Mary James was jerked awake by her blankets being yanked off her. Startled, she watched as the various sheets and linens wafted into the air above her and then fell down. Several of them fell over the man standing at the end of her bed, obscuring him, but when Mary's father, brought by her screams, punched at the shape it collapsed to nothing. Mary swore to everyone the next day that the falling sheets had formed the shape of Dent, although when she was asked how blankets could look like a man, let alone a specific man, she had no proper answer.

Ben Carter saw Dent creeping along Martledge's main street late one night, but as Carter was a thief and a drunk most people dismissed him without much thought. Grace Cole did not; nor did Mary James or Alice Moreby, and when the Manningham baby vanished from its cot in the kitchen in the middle of the day, everyone started to mention Dent's name. It was though a dam had broken, the various stories told recently about sightings of the smiling man swirling and coalescing around the vanished child until, as the police and volunteers searched Martledge and the surrounding areas for any clue as to what might have happened, they formed a patchwork whole that then generated its own reality.

Dent was seen by Emily Cooper skulking in the back garden one along from hers, peering at the upper windows of the houses about him, and her screams brought neighbours and light – it turned out to be a huddled cloth thrown carelessly onto a compost heap and leaning garden fork. He was seen by the river, and the resulting cry brought a small mob of Martledge's concerned citizens to surround a labourer making his innocent way home after a day in the fields, the man narrowly escaping a beating or worse. The resulting furore reached the ears of both police and the clergy, with Reverend Booth preaching about tolerance and the lack of panic from the pulpit the following Sunday, while van Hewson, impassive, watched him from the side of the altar and the police made their presence known by standing at the back of the church and looking around, without accusation but stern nonetheless.

No trace of the Manningham child was ever found, though, and sightings of the dead man continued, some of them less easy to explain. He was seen several times in the churchyard, once by a group of people including a visiting land assessor, who described the odd, smiling man who had watched him as he marked out the cemetery and took various depth samples, to a fault, the description recognisable to those who remembered him as Dent. Other people saw him on the green at night, by the lych gate, where he was seen to move around the structure to ensure he kept in sight an unsuspecting female passer-by, but vanished when people came closer.

By now even the normally unflappable van Hewson was beginning to wonder about the situation and the safety of the people of Martledge, and Booth was panicking because if too much publicity ensued then their actions in making the cemetery a fit space for burial again might be studied in more than cursory detail. "I am happy I have acted within God's grace," said Booth to van Hewson, but he didn't sound convinced and van Hewson shared his misgivings. What had seemed an easy solution was becoming a problem. George Dent was becoming a problem.

Some of the sightings of Dent van Hewson dismissed as hysteria, the thoughtless prattling of flighty girls or feeble men, but other were less inclined to be washed away so easily. As much as he trusted anyone, van Hewson trusted some of the people telling about their sightings of Dent. Grace Cole was sensible and steady, not given to sillinesses of nature or imagination, and even Ben Carter had been sober when he claimed to have seen the dead man. The Manningham child he thought was in the river having been too sickly to live, put there by a father given to rages and impetuosity, but now the rumours of Dent's involvement were creating something new, something unwieldy and dangerous. Something, van Hewson decided, had to be done.

"I never met him," said Booth later that night. Under the guise of a perfectly normal parish business meeting between sexton and vicar, they were discussing the troublesome, dead Dent. Booth's wife had been sent from the room, as she always was, after providing them with refreshments, and the two men had begun to talk.

"There are always rumours, though," replied van Hewson. "Tell me about them."

"I don't listen to gossip or rumour," said Booth pompously, bristling.

"Perhaps you should," said van Hewson. "It might help you understand your parish a little better." It was true; Booth had come here around six years previously from a city parish, and never really fitted in. He seemed to understand little of the natural cycle that the farmers had to exploit, and his fondness for life's niceties had left him open to manipulation by van Hewson in a myriad ways. Both men had done well out of Martledge, though, by accident in Booth's case and design in van Hewson's, and their self-interest meant they had to protect the growing village. The church's coffers needed to stay fat if the two of them were to stay so comfortable.

"I know my predecessor wouldn't bury the man," said Booth suddenly. "I can't remember who told me, but old Scarrow brought someone in from a neighbouring parish to carry out the rites when Dent was buried, although he never explained to anyone why. When they asked, he'd just shake his head and turn away. Scarrow believed in the old ways though, I do remember that. He was always following some nonsensical superstition or other, saluting magpies to ward off bad luck, putting eggshells on the top of his chicken coop to stop the chickens dying, believing that chewing wood from a tree that had been struck by lightning could cure toothache, that sort of thing. He wouldn't marry anyone in May either, nor bury people on the last day in October. I always thought whatever he had against Dent was just another part of that silliness."

Silliness. The folk myths and old wives tales of an area dismissed wholesale as *silliness*, which is why Booth would never fit in anywhere like this. Van Hewson sighed, and tried to think. "So Scarrow didn't like him enough to refuse to bury him, but still let him be buried in the church grounds. Odd, don't you think? Either Scarrow and Dent had some personal furies with each other, or something else was going on for Scarrow to refuse and then to go to the trouble of bringing another vicar in. He'd risk a diocesan enquiry at the very least, wouldn't he?"

"Yes," said Booth after a moment.

"Yet Dent seems to have rested peaceful until only recently?"

"Yes," said Booth, more warily. He was like that, van Hewson knew, not wanting to talk about things in the past that were murky in case they were dragged out into the light, making him look bad. "But there's no connection, surely? Dent can't really be back from the dead, not as spirit nor a flesh and blood thing. Can he?"

"Our Lord came back from the dead, and we

pray to the Holy Ghost," said van Hewson quietly. "If they can do it, who's to say someone else can't as well? The question is, how to make Dent rest again?"

Van Hewson spent some time researching the problem while Booth dithered. He encouraged Booth to pray each night in the cemetery, not because he thought it would work but because it gave the man a focus, something to do, and while Booth bowed his head over his bible, van Hewson bowed his head over the church records.

Scarrow had left a thick box of papers in his will which no one had ever gone through, and with good reason, van Hewson thought after perusing them; they were the dullest diary entries and accounts he had ever read. Scarrow had listed what he had eaten, the weather each day, the notes for his tedious-sounding sermons and his incomings and outgoings, but there was nothing about his parishioners, and nothing about Dent. The man had obviously taken seriously the notion that what he and parishioners spoke about was between the two of them and God. Scarrow, thought van

Hewson, had been about as high as you could get without becoming Catholic, and clearly treated conversations like his Papist counterparts did confessions. *Damn him*, thought van Hewson, who had hoped some simple solution to the growing problem would be found in the papers.

If Scarrow believed in the old ways, maybe the answer was there? So thinking, van Hewson turned to folklore.

There were a bewildering variety of ways to lay the supernatural, he discovered. Apparently, you could whip ghosts out of places by chasing them and flailing at them with a leather strap, or drive them away by burning feathers at night in the places they haunted, or by talking at the ghost until it left through sheer boredom, but he couldn't see these activities going unnoticed in an already on-edge Martledge. Similarly, there was no spilled blood of a murdered man to drive a nail through to prevent the ghost walking. Besides, who knew what Dent actually was? Grace Cole had been very clear that her pursuer, the smiling Dent, had been corporeal, had affected and been affected by the grasses he pushed through. So, ghost or something more?

Did it matter? Dent had been quiet before his

bones were moved, and what did his stone say? *He sleeps in solitary depths*. Was it as simple as that? Had they simply woken him by moving him? And if so, could they send him back aslumber by simply undoing their error? Was it that easy?

He thought it might be, and made plans to find out.

Van Hewson wouldn't let Booth hire labourers to do the job, reasoning that although their silence could be relied upon by the application of coin for the simple job of moving old bones, the atmosphere in Martledge now might unstitch their lips immediately, or failing that, the first time after the task they took a drink, and this needed to stay quiet and hidden. Instead, he and Booth did the deed, first opening Dent's old grave in readiness and then going beyond the wall and digging down through the recently turned and thankfully loose earth of Dent's new resting place and reaching his bones without too much effort. Digging at night was a problem but the moon was bright enough to see by and the trees around the graveyard shielded them from prying eyes. They worked in silence as far as possible, although van Hewson did have a cover story for if they were discovered. *We're digging up his remains to sanctify them*, he'd say, *because we discovered in the old records that Scarrow refused to let him be buried in consecrated ground. His stone is a marker with no bones beneath.* It wouldn't stand up to close scrutiny but most of Martledge would accept it without question, he thought, if it meant Martledge's resident spook was laid away.

Van Hewson saw the figure as they carried the bones around the cemetery wall to the gate. It was over on the green, by the lych gate, and although it was little more than a dark blur in the night, featureless and vague, he knew immediately that it was staring at them.

And smiling.

Van Hewson urged Booth on. Dent's dirty bones, now collected in an old leather satchel, clinked slightly as they went, van Hewson trying to keep Booth's attention away from the figure in case he went to jelly and started screaming. Van Hewson felt like screaming himself because the figure was moving towards them now, fast, loping across the green, and he was reminded of Grace's story about the way it moved through the grass and the speed it had attained, and he recognised it now from the descriptions he'd heard of the man and his smile.

George Dent was chasing them.

He thought they might be safe in the graveyard, it being holy ground, before remembering that Dent's ghost or spirit or restless soul or whatever it was had already been seen in there and sure enough, as they darted along the path to the open grave before Dent's headstone, the shape entered the church grounds behind them with no hesitation. Booth, who still had not seen Dent, resisted van Hewson's pushing, wheezing from the effort of digging, but he pushed the man on. Looking back, he saw that Dent had left the path and was weaving through the graves, darting from one to the other, its shadow a streak across the silvered grass. Van Hewson tried to move faster but he, too, was unhealthy after years of good living, and his legs seemed too slow, too stolid. Dent slipped from one stone to the other, gaining, creeping closer, and now he looked somehow less than human, something angular and distorted yet still smiling that odd little half smile that revealed just a flash of teeth. Van Hewson moaned as the dead man dropped over the top of a nearby stone and oozed along the grass like a limbed snake before disappearing behind the nearby private crypt of one of Martledge's forgotten landowners. *They have seen the glories of His hand*, he remembered the inscription on the outside of the crypt read, and thought, *That's nothing to what I'm seeing*.

They were at the old grave now. Van Hewson wrestled the bag from Booth, opened and upturned it and unceremoniously dropped the contents into the hole. As Booth, a confused look on his face, began to pray over the bones, van Hewson took a spade and started to throw earth in the yawning mouth at his feet. Over Booth's shoulder, he saw Dent emerge from behind the crypt and began to slink towards them, face long and pale in the moonlight, smile ever-present, but his eyes were nothing but blackness, black pools that might have gone on forever, burning and cold and endless, and he shovelled faster as Booth came to the end of the prayer. The last fragment of bone vanished under earth, and van Hewson breathed a sigh of relief. It was done.

Only, if they'd done it, why was Dent still slipping towards them, body naked and thin and smooth like an eel's but white, bone and dust white. Van Hewson couldn't speak, couldn't breathe, as the dead thing grasped Booth from behind.

Booth didn't cry out. Instead, he made a kind of tired, strangled gasp as Dent's face rose up from behind him, the pale hands locked around his throat; was this what he'd wanted all the time, to get revenge on the people who'd woken him, because the look on his, on *its*, face was triumphant, eyes blazing and mouth open and still grinning, a rictus wrench that twisted his face unnaturally about. Van Hewson ran, abandoning Booth and running to where the labourer's tools were piled against the church's rear wall. Somewhere in the pile, he knew, were hammers and long, heavy iron spikes used to repair the fence when it broke. Scrabbling through them, as Booth made a lesser, more terrible sound from behind him, he found the hammer and a spike and started back across the grass to the grave.

Dent was on top of Booth now in an embrace that was almost a lover's, curling around the man. He ignored van Hewson, thank God, so busy was he with Booth. It gave van Hewson time to push the stone at the head of the dead man's grave. Already made unstable by twice having the earth at its feet dug up, the stone wobbled, shifted and then fell, creating a lid over the bones. *No coffin*, thought van Hewson, *no coffin but a stone lid*, and then he was trying to hammer the spike into the stone as Dent finished with Booth and turned towards him.

At the first blow, the spike skidded off the stone and Dent's smile widened into a grin, but with the second blow van Hewson drove the heavy pole into the stone and sent chips up about his head. The stone cracked as he hit it a third time, sparks flying from the spike's head and giving the scene a nightmare light for the briefest moment, Dent stretching out towards him, fingers longer than they should be, tongue drooling from his mouth, skin gleaming and wretched, and then he hit a fourth time and the spike was driven though the stone and into the earth beneath where the bones lay waiting.

Dent stopped, staring at van Hewson, then started to dwindle away, slipping back into the shadows around him, his paleness becoming nothing more than moonlight. His grin fell back to its more usual half-smile and as he vanished, van Hewson was sure the dead man mouthed something at him. Van Hewson took a few seconds, the scene processing through his mind, before realising what the dead man had said.

Dent had said *Thank you*.

Van Hewson slumped over Dent's fractured, impaled grave and waited for the sun to come. It started to rain, a summer storm, and bones emerged from the earth like new, tender shoots.

~

He'd had to come out in the end, away from the computer and the temptation it provided.

The green was busy, the sun having summoned children and mothers and dogs, and there were at least three separate picnics taking place on it, while in the middle a rag-tag, apparently formless game of football was taking place between two ever-shifting teams of children of all ages. Nakata found a space against the lych gate and sat, enjoying the sun on his face. He had a paperback book in his pocket but decided against reading – it suddenly seemed like too much effort. Instead, he drifted.

The sounds of the game and the chatter of the people around him faded as Nakata let himself doze. He emptied his head of ghosts, of his father and mother, of Amy, of the things that had happened and the hopes he had, and let himself for the first time in a long time simply *be*. He was Richard Nakata, and he was alive, and for now, that was enough.

A shadow crossed over him, momentarily blocking the sun's heat and he shivered, but didn't open his eyes. In the distance he heard a few bars of music, floating and serene, and then it was gone. Water splashed, rippling, and someone laughed, low and earthy and sultry. Nakata smiled.

Tomorrow, he would start the next phase of his experiment but in that moment, he was at peace.

~

The Meadows

They waited until dusk when the Meadows were emptying, and then they went in.

Rather than park in the car park by the information centre and now-closed ice-cream kiosk, they parked on one of the little roads in the Ville. Having found the gently sloping path that led down through the tree-shrouded lane, they came out above fields that had once been farmland, but which were now part of the vast, sprawling nature reserve. Bethany held Luke's hand as they walked and the wine bottle in the bag over his shoulder clinked amiably against the glasses, making a sound like birds chirruping.

In the falling dusk and rising moon the Meadows were painted in shades of grey, the river a dark thread just visible beyond the flood barrier, the lights of The Spearman's Boat glimmering in the distance. Bethany loved it here, loved the peace of it and the smell of it and the sound of it, a low buzz of insects and small animals rustling through the grass. The path lay ahead of them, branching and coming back together at points, taking them past fields that were fenced in, to protect the wild growth within, and others that were open for use. Half a mile or so upstream, where the river turned towards Martledge, an artificial body of water had been created; not quite large enough to be called a lake but bigger than a pond. People called it Martledge Tarn, home to wild birds and fish, the path around it used by runners, mothers with buggies wanting their children to get some fresh air, and walkers who wanted to walk through nature.

And, at night, by lovers.

"It's beautiful," said Luke, and sounded like he meant it, thereby passing the first of Bethany's unspoken relationship tests. Her boyfriends had to like the Meadows, had to love it the way she did, before she would contemplate anything more than a casual moment with them. She didn't let Luke see that she was happy he had passed; she liked him a lot, but it wouldn't do for him to realise how much, not yet anyway. She led him down the path and then up to the top of the flood barrier where a wide path had been edged in wood, the earth gravelled and flat. Closer to, the river sounded like it was chuckling to itself, as though it had secrets that it would never tell. It was a sound that never failed to make her smile, and she was pleased to see Luke smile when he heard it too. It wasn't another unspoken test, but it was definitely a bonus point in his favour.

"What's that?" he asked as they strolled along. Bethany's hand was damp in his, not just because of the night's heat but because she was sure now what they would do when they reached their destination. They had wine, and a blanket, and the night was warm and the moon was high and near full, giving them all the light they needed, and Luke was handsome and kind and funny and hers, and this was what she wanted. Luke was looking at a marker of some kind that had been placed by the side of the path, an angled plaque on top of a wooden stake.

"I don't know," she replied, and the two of them crossed the path to see the marker. She hadn't been to the Meadows for several months because of being away at university, and this hadn't been here when she last came.

The plaque, a piece of wood with either plastic or laminated card attached to it, it was hard to tell, had been placed on the path by the Martledge Water Park Authority, and it was part of a trail of information boards that apparently ran the length of the path. This one was numbered '6' and listed some of the fish that lived in the river and animals that lived on or near the banks. There was a tiny picture of a vole, another of a rat, one of a churned mess of eels and several more of fish. Luke read the information with a rapt look on his face. He lived in an industrial town, and had joked with her the first time they met that the greenest thing he saw was the anti-vandal paint on top of the local park's railings. They carried on and soon enough they came to another plaque, this one with a drawing of a fisherman dressed in rough clothing, clearly dating from the eighteenth century or earlier. The information on the plaque talked about how the river sustained the local community, providing irrigation and food. The next plaque showed farmers working the fields, and the one after talked about flooding and was illustrated with a drawing of the area covered in a silvery, flat mass of water out of which an occasional tree or hedgerow protruded. They read each plaque together, and then talked about a series of nothings as they walked, a slight, pleasurable tension growing between them.

The last plaque before the lake that wasn't a lake showed birds that nested in the Meadows and how to recognise them but by then the Tarn was in sight and the lights of the Spearman were far behind them and a heat was growing in Bethany; she wanted to find them somewhere dark and shaded and put the blanket down and get the wine and glasses out of the bag and be everything in Luke's world, even if only for a few minutes. She did not care about birds or eels or farming or floods, there was just the heat and the need and the urgency and the night giving them cover and secrecy.

After, they lay on the blanket, not talking. Luke reached out and held Bethany's hand but unlike before when it had felt as though their contact was exploratory, testing each other out, now it was possessive in the best way, not a contact of ownership but of belonging to each other, she hoped. Eventually, she disentangled their fingers and sat up, pulling her skirt down. Luke, next to her, sat up and tugged his shirt back up around his shoulders and then leaned over to kiss her, long and slow and dreamy. "We should be going," she said. "It's getting late and cold."

"Is it cold? I'd not noticed," said Luke, pulling back so that she could see his face. He was grinning lazily, content, and she had a suddenly burst of wild despair that he might not feel the same as her, that this might be something transient and unimportant. Maybe he saw the thought on her face because he leaned forward and kissed her again, and breathed the words, "I'm warm enough with you, let's stay a while," into her mouth.

They had wine left so they poured it out and sat, rearranging clothing and listening to the Meadows move into the night around them. The water in front of them chattered to the river behind them, nocturnal animals moved around in the darkness, hunting or being hunted. They were on the slope that formed between the water and the flank of the flood bank, close to a copse of small trees, and the stars above them were hard points of white set into the velvet roll of the sky. Bethany thought that her life had, maybe, never been as perfect.

The sound of the river changed, picking up a rhythmic *thwock* and *plunk* beat, a new punctuation in its grammar. Luke glanced back up the slope and said, "That's a boat."

It surprised her. Luke was a city boy who claimed never to have spent time in the countryside. He saw her looking at him with the question in her eyes and said, "We have water in cities, Bethany. There was a boating lake near where I grew up, we used to go when I was a kid. That's the sound of water against the side of a wooden boat. It's not quite the same noise as I used to hear then, but it's close enough." He stood, brushing down his jeans and then holding his hand out to her.

"Shall we?"

"What?"

"Go and see?"

She was going to say no, someone might see them, but then realised it didn't matter if they did. They were adults, they'd done no harm and they were allowed to be here. She reached out and took his hand again and he hauled her up, pulling her to him accidentally on purpose and stealing a kiss as he did so. The wine had made her feel fuzzy, pleasantly so, and she wished life could be like this forever, even though she was enough of a realist to know it could not. Luke picked up the bag, put the glasses and now empty bottle inside it and then the two of them went to the top of the bank.

The river was empty of boats.

As they watched, the water continued its meandering flow that would take it, thirty miles or so downstream, to the coast and the open ocean beyond. There was another series of hollow sounds, of wood tapped by wavelets, and then another sound, a creak and groan of wood moving against a current. Bethany caught a whiff of something sharp and acrid that made her think of engines and then it was gone, and a voice, clear and loud, called out, "Mind that fucking load! It's fucking shifting!"

Luke jumped at the voice and his hand tightened on hers, almost painfully, so that she had to pull away, and as she did so a second voice said, "Christ, what's he doing now?" There was a booming sound and a deeper *thunk* and Bethany swore the earth shook under her, and that for a moment she saw a dark shape plough up against the bank and then fall away, but it could only have been a shadow, a bubble of cloud crossing the moon maybe, because moments later the river was clear again.

"Can you smell that?" asked Luke and Bethany was about to answer no, but then she could, not the engine odour of before but whiskey, strong and sharp and rough, not the elegant, peaty nose of the single malt her father sometimes drank. She looked at Luke and his eyes saucered in the night, and she thought her eyes were probably doing the same.

"Holy Christ!" shouted a voice – without a body, without presence – and it sounded like the first voice but louder, more raw, hovering somewhere between anger and fear. There was a sloshing sound, and the deep, hollow boom of water slapping against wood, and the surface of the water suddenly roiled. There was a shaking from under Bethany's feet and then a wave splashed back from a point on the far bank, from a specific point, and again she thought she saw a dark shadow, huge and wavering, that was gone as soon as it came.

Someone screamed.

There were a series of creaks, the sound of things snapping and tumbling, splashes as things they couldn't see fell into the water, more screams, a shout and a curse and then the terrible noise of water swirling and bubbling, of wood straining and snapping and of men splashing. Then, worse, there was the sound of the earth itself tearing and Luke shrieked and started down the slope. Now Bethany could hear it too, the sound of men trying to scramble up the steep slope, and of a boat half rolled and dragging along the bank, its deck now vertical, wheelhouse roof also dragging into the bank because it was now on its side and half in the water, horizontal, prow and wheelhouse catching the men and tearing them back into the water, breaking them as it did so.

Another noise, of air rupturing out of torn wood, the water's surface splitting and popping, more things falling, more screaming but this time choking too, another curse, a reek of chemicals that came and went on a breeze that Bethany didn't feel and then more splashes, the sound of people trying to swim. Luke was at the edge of the river now, balancing precariously on the slope and looking across the water. The water's surface was choppy but still there was nothing to be seen, no men or boat, but the *plunk plunk* of the water hitting wood with air behind it continued, although the sounds got deeper, less hollow, with each beat, as though the space was filling quickly.

Someone cried out, a wet howl in the darkness, the single word "Help" that rose and then trailed off in a gurgle.

A bang as two somethings crashed into each other, and then the long, dead noise of a keel dragging along the bank a while further before coming away with a wet sucking sound. More water, more cries, and then just the popping of air and, finally, silence.

Bethany's legs collapsed under her and she sat, hard, jarring her teeth together. Luke saw and came back up the slope, his face whey-pale in the night; he took her in his arms and he was warm and solid and real and she began to cry. She thought Luke might be crying too, but didn't pull her face back from his neck to look.

The river sounded normal again, that's what told Bethany that it was over. There was no hollow sound, no wooden tap, just the sound of it giggling to itself as it flowed slowly on, and that realisation brought her tears to an end. She finally pulled back from Luke, not really wanting to because, even under these circumstances, the feel of him against her was thrilling, and they stood. At some point the bag had rolled down the slope and was just at the water's edge, so Luke retrieved it and they started back along the path towards the car and the lights of Martledge. They walked in silence.

They had passed two of the information plaques when Luke stopped, stopping Bethany, and said, "What was it?"

"I don't know," said Bethany, but wondered if that was exactly true.

"Something in the wine?" Luke smiled as he said this but the smile didn't quite climb as far as his eyes. She loved him for trying, though.

"That'd be some wine," she replied, also trying to smile, "making us hear ghosts."

"That's what you think it was? Ghosts of—" Luke stopped and his mouth dropped open, a second moon in the night, this one lined by lips that were pale and teeth that were bright and even.

"What?" asked Bethany, but Luke simply

raised a hand in response, his mouth becoming, if possible, even rounder.

Bethany turned and saw them. There were figures crawling up the bank.

Actually, they weren't figures so much as shapes, as though five people were casting shadows across the earth but were somehow invisible themselves, so that only the blackened and featureless suggestions of them remained. They were stretched out along the grass verge as though on their hands and knees, heads low, arms grasping forwards, legs digging and kicking, driving themselves up the slope. One was ahead of the others, the four behind it in a block that that it looked like the first was harnessed, was pulling them. They were silent as they inched up the slope.

Neither Luke nor Bethany moved. Luke's arm dropped and they stood next to each other, a silent audience to a silent show. The five figures moved labouriously, the effort obvious in the way that they seemed to drag and rock as they came on. When the lead figure reached the top of the bank it carried on crawling, an image that seemed to have no depth or solidity because the figures themselves had no solidity, were only a shadow of something not there.

The four trailing figures came over the lip of the bank as the lead figure rose unsteadily to its feet. Moments later the other four followed, and although they had no features, Bethany thought they were facing Luke and her. She stepped back, bumping into Luke, who put his arms on her shoulders and moved her gently, to the side of the path but not away. The lead figure paused as though gathering itself then moved, swaying unevenly from side to side, its gait almost a stagger as it came towards them. A moment after it started moving the others followed, and although they were as slow as the first their movement was more even, less disjointed. Their shapes though, Bethany saw, were more damaged that the first. One had an arm sticking out from its body at a petulant, jutting angle and another's head, or what she assumed was its head, was wrenched to one side and down, apparently unable to straighten up. The rearmost figure's trailing leg seemed twisted and somehow mangled, knee buckled and foot bent the wrong way around so it pointed backward as it came on, as though to indicate where it had been rather than where it was going. None of the figures acknowledged Bethany or Luke.

The first figure came abreast of them. Bethany took another step back, couldn't help herself, and this time Luke did too, and she felt herself taking a step off the bank, teetering slightly before finding her footing. Luke was behind her, using her shoulders to steady himself and now she could hear something, just faintly, the sound of water dripping and spattering, and although the figure was still a vaguely man-shaped shadow she knew that river water was dripping off it and falling, unseen, to the earth at its feet. When its followers got close enough she heard the dripping from them too, an uneven tattoo of taps and spots, along with a thick, sluicing sound that she thought was soaked cloth dragging across skin and against other cloth as the figures moved.

"It's the sailors," Luke whispered, "the ones we heard before." A statement, not a question.

"Yes," said Bethany, because who else could they be?

The first figure was almost past them now but turned its head to look at them as it went, acknowledging them for the first time, and although he had no features Bethany thought he was anguished, that if she could have seen his face it would have been twisted into a mask of misery. She smelled something, not the engine but the whiskey again, strong and sour. The figure turned away from them, looking again at the path ahead and took another wretched, lumbering staggering step.

The first of the followers was at them now, arm sticking out to the side as though pointing at something on the far side of the river. There was no smell of whiskey but a rank whiff of river water, of dirt and something that might have been blood.

The second, and the overriding smell was of vomit. This figure was breathing, or trying to through its yanked neck, the sounds a steam kettle whistle of air, blocked and straining. The sound was awful, painful and pitiful and lost, and it made Bethany's throat tighten in sympathy and horror and she wanted to cry out but didn't, couldn't.

The third, which didn't at first appear to be physically wrong (*apart from being a shadow, a moving shadow*, thought Bethany almost hysterically, *it's fine apart from that*) but then the smell hit, of blood and excrement, and the sound of dragging, and Bethany could suddenly see loops of shadow intestine dropping and trailing by the figure's legs and pulling through the dirt, and this time she did cry out, a little mewl that sounded as unlike her as any noise she had ever made, and the figure's head turned and the expression on the face she couldn't see was more terrible than that of the first figure's, agonised and hopeless and betrayed and ruined.

The fourth, the last thank God, the one with the trailing leg and twisted foot. This one was almost easy to bear after the previous figure, the injuries to it almost casually dreadful but not so awful. This one didn't smell either, and made no sound, and it did not turn to look at Bethany or Luke as it passed.

Once the figures were fully past them Bethany and Luke stepped back off the slope and onto the path together .They watched the shapes as they continued shambling down the path, slow and uneven but inexorable, not stopping until they reached a patch of natural shadow, the shadow cast by the trees she and Luke had so recently lain beneath, realised Bethany, and then they faded. It took a few moments, was as slow a disappearance as their movements had been, their edges shifting and blurring, spreading, drawing out into the dark air around them until there was nothing left of them. Bethany realised that there were tears streaming down her face and that there probably had been for minutes now, and when she turned to Luke she saw that he was crying too. She let out a breath that she hadn't realised she was holding and turned back to the path. The figures hadn't returned, and the night around them was thankfully, wonderfully normal.

Nearby, there was the sound of flapping wings and something small and natural shrieked its death. The sound broke the spell and the two of them were looking at each other and talking together, over each other.

"What the—"

"Did you—"

"I'm sorry," said Luke, "you first."

"You're right, it was the sailors that we heard, riverboat men or something, they'd been in the water and they were wet, were dripping."

"Yes," said Luke, almost excited, "but what were they doing?"

"Following the first one," said Bethany.

"But not because they wanted to. They seemed tied to him in some way, like he was dragging them," and Bethany remembering her thought about the first figure, *man* she supposed she had to think if it as, being harnessed to the ones behind him and nodded. "But why?"

Instead of answering, Luke set off along the path. Bethany, after a moment, followed, wary but not wanting to lose sight or hold of him. Luke slowed as he reached the shadows of the trees, glanced down the slope to where they had been before and then along the path. After a second, he dug his phone out of his pocket.

"I never thought of it until now," he said, almost apologetic.

"It wouldn't have recorded anything," she replied, knowing that was true without knowing how.

"No,' he agreed, then flicked on the phone's torch application and sent the weak beam into the shadows.

Just a path, hard packed, making its way under the overhanging branches of a copse of trees, the river to the other side flowing, minding its own business.

"What's that?" Bethany asked, pointing to a shape in the darkness at the side of the path.

Now the world had righted itself and the immediacy of her fear was retreating she was becoming wildly curious. The universe had opened a door tonight and she had to look through to see what was on the other side, might even have to step through if that's where the answers were.

"It's one of those information signs," said Luke and they went to it together.

The plaque was like the others, some printed text and a drawing, although this one was less colourful than the others they had seen. *This plaque marks the spot*, it read, *where the river barge The Reynard crashed into the bank and rolled, spilling its crew and cargo into the water and drowning them before sinking.* Below the information was a date.

"He was drunk, and he crashed the barge," said Bethany, toneless with the realisation of it, of the thing the leading man, the barge's captain, had done. He had killed them all.

"And now they're tied to him forever," replied Luke in the same tone, "always following him into their endings, following him after that because they haven't any other thing to do."

"He was drunk, and he killed them," said Bethany again, and thought of those four figures ever chasing the first, ever trying to catch him so that they might break the links that bound them.

"Look," said Luke, pointing at the date on the plaque. "It was two hundred years ago it happened. Maybe that's why there here, it's an anniversary and they're living their deaths out again."

"No," said Bethany, feeling fresh tears prickle at her, "they're always here, all the time, we just saw them for some reason. They're dying here all the time."

"Yes," said Luke, as the noise of the river changed and the sound of water slapping against the hull of a boat reached their ears once more.

~

He'd given it two weeks.

By now, he knew, the comments were mounting up behind each story and there were a number of threads open in the discussion area of the site. Nakata still hadn't read any of them but he had monitored them from a distance, and was confident that at least some of them were adding to the stories he had published. He would read everything later. First, though, he was going walkabout.

Nakata lived in one of the newer developments of Martledge, in a suburb built on land that had been open fields until the 1950s; he knew because he'd researched the property and the history of it and the site it stood on before he bought it. He might approach the idea of ghosts scientifically, and have what he felt were sound theories as to their origin and even how they existed, but all the same he had no urge to live somewhere built on an old graveyard, or somewhere that had been the site of a mass murder. He didn't consider himself psychic, not exactly, but sometimes thought a supernatural experience was a little like herpes; once there, it never completely went away and left you at risk of reinfection under certain circumstances. "Well," he said out loud to himself the first time he'd thought this, "maybe not herpes, maybe it's more like having malaria and the risk of it recurring is always there. It leaves you susceptible somehow."

He still thought of ghosts as a little like herpes though.

Nakata recognised a kind of giddiness in himself as he left the house. It was the excitement that always came with the start of the practical part of the work, whether that was sitting motionless in the haunted house, the interviewing of witnesses and sceptics or, as now, going to walk the various places into which he'd inserted ghosts. This movement, from intellectual to physical action, always marked the point at which he moved from one stage to another, marked progression and movement and hopefully, the beginning of success. All the questions, all the steps taken, leading to more and those steps to more and those to yet more again, on and ever on – it was what he loved because, ultimately, this was who he was, wasn't it? Always asking, always wanting to know?

Yes. This was him, and accepting that – or rather re-accepting it after the uncertainty of these last few months – felt good. *Maybe I'm healing,* he thought, *not healed yet, but healing, although I'm not sure what my injuries were, not exactly. A loss of faith, maybe? A punctured confidence?*

Spiritual herpes?

Stifling the giggle that threatened to emerge from him and turn into a guffaw, Nakata walked to what everyone considered the centre of Martledge, the green – even if, at only a few minutes' walk from the upper reached of the Meadows, it was geographically closer to the western edge of the town than the centre. It was only a short stroll to get there and he enjoyed the warmth of the summer air as he went, the falling night that shrouded around him. Martledge was quiet but not dead, the Horse and Jockey and The George pubs letting a low murmur and music and light into the air. Nakata ignored them, and went first to the south end of the Green, through the lych gate and onto the road beyond. An old, now empty house with a large yard locally called 'Minahane's Yard' stood just beyond the road. It was where he had set the first of his stories, and it was where he had chosen to start tonight. Nakata stood in the centre of the yard and waited.

There was a distant tinkle of a piano riff, something slow, carried on the air from the pub but nothing else.

Nakata was disappointed, and annoyed with himself for the disappointment. *What did you expect*, he asked himself? *The ghost of an old lady who'd come and tell you exactly how she existed just because you found a story about her in the town archives and then tried to write her into existence?*

Next he went to the church, passing back through the lych gate as he went. Someone was standing in the shadows of the far side of the gate, a drinker from the pub he thought, maybe a smoker or someone on a phone call that was private, so he hurried past them and did not look closely for fear of offending or intruding. The green was dark now, the concrete path under his feet a streak of heavy grey in the night that took him to the far gate and then over the road into St Clements' churchyard.

Here, again, was nothing. Nakata wandered about for several minutes but saw nothing except a gravestone lying flat to the earth towards the back wall, behind the church. It seemed to have a metal stake hammered through it, cut down low so that it didn't stick up, which he didn't think he'd noticed before. He certainly didn't remember it. The grass that curled over the edge of the grave, although newly cut, was oddly thin and straggly around the old stone's edges and the inscription on the stone had been worn away by years of rain and feet. He thought he heard rain falling, just a little, and noted it in his reporter's notebook, putting the time next to the note. Even though he could hear them, he could feel no drops, and there was nothing else.

Leaving St Clements, Nakata retraced his steps. The person was still standing by the lych gate, but this time they deliberately kept the gate between Nakata and themselves, moving around it so that Nakata could hear them but not see them, wanting to stay hidden and private. He followed the road, soon reaching the Meadows and shortly after, the flood bank.

Still nothing.

Sighing, Nakata took the printout of the web page from his pocket, unfolded it, smoothed the creases out and reread it.

Story 1: A retired farmer living just by Martledge Green bought the property of his neighbour, an elderly recluse called Ellie Whinfell, after her death. Some of it he gave away or burned but some of her nicer furniture he kept in his own home, only to find that Ellie wasn't ready to move on. Ellie began to appear in the man's home, using her furniture, moving things around in the night and making noises from downstairs until the only way he could stop it was to burn the items of Ellie's that he still owned.

Story 2: George Dent, who had lived and died in Martledge in the mid-nineteenth century, had his grave disturbed twenty years after his death and was subsequently seen by a number of people in and around the green or looking in people's windows. He only stopped appearing when his grave was put back to its original state.

Story 3: A young couple enjoying an evening together in the Meadows heard the ghosts of riverboat men who drowned when their river barge rolled over and sank. The men had drowned because the cargo on the barge's deck had been incorrectly stowed by the captain, a drunk, and it shifted and listed when the captain took the barge around a river bend too quickly, causing the

barge to roll. The couple swear they heard voices, heard
the sound of the boat going down, and that they had
not been drinking.

Nakata refolded the page and put it back in his pocket. Had his stories grown? Had people added to them, made them more? It was time, he thought, to find out. He turned to go back, seeing in the distance a solitary figure walking from Martledge along the path towards him, and hearing piano music again. From somewhere behind him, Nakata heard the hollow, echoing slap of water against wood and thought that a boat was probably moored nearby.

This, then, is Martledge.

It has ghosts, and they are making for Nakata.

~

Story Notes

A bit of history, seeing as history seems to have become a theme in these stories without, as ever, me intending for it to happen: the version first version of Nakata I wrote was as a secondary character in a (thankfully still unpublished) novel. He was older and less personable than the version I created later for my collection, *Quiet Houses*, but even then I liked him. He was driven and honest and capable of facing down ghosts while helping that story's hero achieve his end. This Nakata was an academic (that's remained constant) but he was older, more aloof and less willing to flex and bend and roll with the punches. I did a terrible thing to that Nakata, but I did it off-screen (as it were) and I've never worked out what the terrible thing was, only that it scarred that Nakata and left him damaged.

Jump forward a few years. Having agreed to write a portmanteau collection, I was casting around for a linking character when I remembered Nakata, which had always seemed a better person to revisit than the hero (who was, I am ashamed to admit, fairly bland). I changed his name, shaved a few years off him and wrote him as well as I could. I put him through the ringer, made him dance and jerk to my puppet master's manipulations, and found in doing so that occasionally he would surprise me, would go off in directions I hadn't anticipated. I liked even more this Nakata, the one of *Quiet Houses*, who'd had some of his rougher edges smoothed off and who seemed to me to represent all the things a good hero should be: inquisitive, fallible, weary, bruised, brave and smart. I left him in a strange place, personally and professionally, but I always wanted to revisit him to see how he'd got on after the events of *Quiet Houses* because he felt like he *should* be revisited. I got caught up in writing novels after that, though, so never really had the chance until 2016, when I got to talk with him again in a one-off story called 'The Terrible Deaths of the Ghosts of the Westmorland' (the final story in my collection *Diseases of the Teeth*). Despite the time lapse, I found that I still liked Nakata a lot and wanted to know more about him...or at least, to put him in yet more danger.

Which brings us to *The Martledge Variations*. When Steve Shaw (grand master and whip wielder of Black Shuck Books) asked if I'd write a micro collection for his Shadows series, my immediate response was that I would, but only if it could be a Nakata collection, which thankfully he agreed to (sensible chap!). It was time to visit my friend again, to see where he'd come to. Not far, I thought, but he'd definitely have moved. The question was, where to?

And the answer was Martledge.

I started to think about places, which had always featured so heavily in the first Nakata stories, and a set of half-formed ideas in my head merged with some of the information I'd just read in the fabulous book, *The Quirks of Chorlton-cum-Hardy* (by Andrew Simpson & Peter Topping[1]), about the town where I grew

~~~

[1] *The Quirks of Chorlton-cum-Hardy: A History of Its People and Places*, Andrew Simpson and Peter Topping, Topper Publishing, 2017 - if you have any connect with Chorlton at all, I can't recommend this

up, and out of the random mess in my head a set of linked stories were born. I'd steal Chorlton's history, I decided, and put Nakata slap bang in the middle of it all. So I did. Along the way I dragged in the work of the Owen Group, whose ghostly Philip is a direct ancestor of the characters in these stories, some of the history of Kendal, and snippets of information and myth about other areas of the Lake District to create my Martledge. Martledge, incidentally, is the original name for a part of what is now Chorlton, and the geography of the town in the stories is a corrupted version of the geography of the real Chorlton. There is a real lych gate and green, The Meadows (or Martledge Water Park, to give it its official title) is real, the church and pubs are real. The maypole dancers were real, as was the teacher who created their dances and encouraged even the youngest of children to put on dazzling, complex displays as intricate as anything done by adults. The three men from the bail hostel existed, unfortunately, but so

~~~

book highly enough. It's a wonderful roll (wallow, really) in Chorlton's history and personality, it's well researched and informative and it features people I used to know.

more fortunately so do all the good things, the things that made it a decent place to grow up. Martledge is a nice little town; so is Chorlton.

~

The Dancers

The opening scene if this story is, almost exactly, a recreation of a morning's work I did a few months before writing it, when in the middle of the heaviest snow fall the Lake District had had for several years, I dragged a piano from a barn and took it to pieces with a lump hammer. It was hugely exhilarating, massively noisy work, both cathartic and strangely guilt-inducing (I felt like a savage, killing an instrument capable of such beauty but it was beyond saving because mice had nested in its guts for year and the people I was working for needed their barn clearing), made all the more fun by the fact I got to burn the remains afterwards (don't worry, I made sure the mice were gone first). While I did this fabulous thing (and was paid for it!) I was under the baleful gaze of a collapsing house on the far side of the road and I suddenly thought, what if the piano had come from there, and what if the person destroying the piano wasn't being paid to do so? Why would they beat a piano to death with a lump hammer in a snowstorm? What possible reason could there be?

This story is what I came up with to explain it all.

~

The Smiling Man

Where Chorlton and other places meet... Most of the details about the over-filled ground of the church yard and of bones being washed free every time it rained are true, lifted from Chorlton's history and deposited unceremoniously here, but the smiling man is based (loosely) on another piece of history (or myth, or mythic history), that of the Dent Vampire. Dent is a small village about 75 miles north of Chorlton, and in its church yard is a grave with a stake through it which was done to pin a local vampire to the soil and stop him walking. I wanted to blend these two disparate histories, make them into a single Martledge event, and this is the result.

~

The Meadows

Another one with a bit of everything thrown into the mix. The Meadows are real, as is the water park (called, rather prosaically, The Chorlton Water Park). As far as I know, there was never a boat that sank in the river around there but there is a pub (Jackson's Boat), and it is a great place to go walking or, as in Bethany and Luke's case, lovin' (not that I've done that myself, you understand). When I was a kid we'd go digging for old bottles there, finding some beautiful old pharmacy glass that's still on a shelf in my granddad's house, and as an adult I used to run around the lake that isn't a lake (in actuality a reclaimed gravel pit) in the hope of getting healthy, and on each loop around it I'd see something new: once, a group of mums jogging on the spot with their babies in buggies before them, once a family practicing Tai Chi together, once two drunk people trying to barbeque something that was already black and burning. Luke and Bethany had a bad experience on the meadows but I never did, and if you go there I'd hope you won't too. Its ghosts are, I suspect, gentle and calm. You know the sort? That's right, the ones that Nakata rarely meets...

So, here it is then. Another Nakata collection done and gone, and I've had as much fun with him this time as I did the first, and I hope you have too. Nakata is a decent man in a mostly decent world, and I enjoy his company immensely. I've said it before and I'll say it again, I like Nakata. He'll be back. This time, though, I can add: I'm not done with Martledge yet.

Also by Simon Kurt Unsworth:

Novels
The Devil's Detective (Del Ray / Doubleday, 2015)
The Devil's Evidence (Del Ray / Doubleday, 2016)

Collections
Lost Places (Ash Tree Press, 2010)
Quiet Houses (Dark Continents Publishing, 2011)
Strange Gateways (PS Publishing, 2014)
Diseases of the Teeth (Black Shuck Books, 2016)

Visit Simon Kurt Unsworth at his website:
simonkurtunsworth.wordpress.com

Now available and forthcoming from
Black Shuck Shadows:

blackshuckbooks.co.uk/shadows

Lightning Source UK Ltd.
Milton Keynes UK
UKHW021821130922
408810UK00009B/1417